AF261028

Pee-Wee Harris

by Percy Keese Fitzhugh

Copyright © 8/6/2015
Jefferson Publication

ISBN-13: 978-1515386773

Printed in the United States of America

Contents

CHAPTER I

PEE-WEE HARRIS, mascot of the Raven Patrol, First Bridgeboro Troop, sat upon the lowest limb of the tree in front of his home eating a banana. To maintain his balance it was necessary for him to keep a tight hold with one hand on a knotty projection of the trunk while with the other he clutched his luscious refreshment.

The safety of his small form as he sat on the shaky limb depended upon his hold of the trunk, while the tremendous responsibility of holding his banana devolved upon the other hand.

Pee-wee was so much smaller than he should have been and the banana so much larger than it should have been that they might almost be said to have been of the same size.

The slender limb on which Pee-wee sat trembled and creaked with each enormous bite that he took. The bright morning sunlight, wriggling through the foliage overhead, picked out the round face and curly hair of our young hero and showed him in all his pristine glory, frowning a terrible frown, clinging for dear life with one hand and engaged in his customary occupation of eating.

He had ascended to this leafy throne with the banana in his pocket but he could not restore it to his pocket now even if he wished to. However, he did not wish to. In a military sense he was in a predicament, both arms were in bad strategic position and his center exposed to assault. His leafy throne was like many another throne in these eventful times—extremely shaky.

But the commissary department was in fine shape....

Suddenly the expeditionary forces of Uncle Sam appeared in the form of the postman, who paused on his way across the lawn to the house.

"Hello, up there," he said, suddenly discovering Pee-wee.

"Hello yourself and see how you like it," the mascot of the Ravens called down.

"I saw a banana up there and I thought maybe you were behind it," the postman called, as he looked among the pack of letters he held in his hand.

"It's only half a banana," Pee-wee shouted.

"Well, you're only half a scout," the postman said; "you'd better drop it, here's a letter for you."

"For me?"

"For you."

Steadying himself, Pee-wee took an enormous bite, considerably reducing the length of the banana. "Wait a minute till I finish it," he said as best he could with his mouth full. "Waaer—mint."

"Can't wait," the postman said, heartlessly moving away.

"Waymnt," Pee-wee yelled, frantically taking another bite; "wayermntdyehear, waymnt!"

"Do you think the government can wait for you to finish a banana?" the postman demanded with a wicked grin upon his face. "You got two hands; here, take the letter if you want it; here it is," he added, reaching up.

Pee-wee tried to dispatch the remainder of the banana by one gigantic and triumphant bite but the desperate expedient did not work; his mouth with all its long practice, could not keep up with his hand; it became clogged while yet a considerable length of banana projected out of the gracefully drooping rind.

"Here, take it," the postman said in a tone of ruthless finality.

Chewing frantically and waving the remainder of banana menacingly like a club, the baffled hero uttered some incomprehensible, imploring jumble of suffocated words while the postman moved away a step or two, repressing a fiendish smile.

"Throwaway the banana," he said.

By this time Pee-wee was able to speak and while his chewing apparatus was momentarily disengaged he demanded to know if the postman thought he was crazy. The postman, resolved not to miss the fun of the situation, was not going to let Pee-wee take another bite; time was precious, and two more bites of the sort that Pee-wee took might leave his hand free.

"Take the letter," he said with an air of cold determination, "or I'll leave it at the house. Here, take it quick; I've no time to waste."

"Do you want me to waste a banana," Pee-wee yelled imploringly; "a scout is supposed—"

"Here, take it", the postman said.

There followed the most terrible moment in the life of Pee-wee Harris, Scout. He knew that one more bite would be fatal, that the postman would not wait. In two bites, or in three at most, he could finish the banana and his hand would be free.

How could a postman, who brings joy to the lonely, words of love from far away, cheer to those who wait, comfort from across the seas, Boys' Life Magazine—how could such a being be so relentless and cruel? If that letter were left at the house, Pee-wee would have to go to the house and get it, and there his mother was lying in ambush waiting to pounce upon him and make him mow the lawn, Why would not the postman wait for just two bites? Maybe he could do it in one, he had consumed a peach in one bite and a ham sandwich in four— his star record.

He made a movement with his hand, and simultaneously the postman retreated a step or two toward the house. Pee-wee tried releasing his hold upon the trunk with the other hand and almost lost his balance on the shaky limb.

"Here," said the postman, unyielding, "chuck the banana and take the letter or you'll find it waiting for you in the front hall. It's an important letter, it feels as if it had a couple of cookies in it." The postman knew Pee-wee. "Here you go," the torturer said grimly, "take it or not, suit yourself."

"Can't you see both hands are busy?" the victim pled. "Two bites—a scout is supposed not to waste anything—he's supposed—he's supposed—wait a minute—he's supposed if he starts a thing to finish it—wait, I'm not going to take a bite, I'm only giving you an argument—can't you wait—"

"Here you go, last chance, take it," the postman said, a faint smile hovering at the corner of his mouth, "one, two—"

Out of Pee-wee's wrath and anguish came an inspiration.

"Stick the letter in the banana," he said, holding the banana down.

"I don't know about that," the postman said, ruefully.

"I know about it," Pee-wee thundered down at him. "You said I had to take it or not; that letter belongs to me and you, have to deliver it. This banana, it's—it's the same as a mail box—you stick the letter in the banana. You think you're so smart, you thought you'd make me throw away the banana, naaah, didn't you? I wouldn't do that, not even for—for—secretary—for the postmaster—general, I wouldn't! A scout has resource."

"All right, you win," said the postman, good humoredly, "only look out you don't fall; here you go, hold on tight."

Clutching to the knotty projection of trunk, Pee-wee reached the other hand as low as he could and the postman, smiling, stuck the corner of the coveted letter into the mealy substance of the banana.

"You win," the postman repeated laughingly; "it shows what Scout Harris can do with food."

"Food will win the war," Pee-wee shouted. "You thought you could make me throwaway my banana but you couldn't. I knew a man that died from not eating a banana, I did."

"Explain all that," the postman said.

"He threw a banana away on his porch instead of eating it and later he stepped on it and slid down the steps and broke his leg and they took him to the hospital and compilations set in and he got pneumonia and died from not eating that banana. So there."

"That's a very fine argument." the postman said as he went away.

"I know better ones than that." Pee-wee shouted after him.

CHAPTER II

A TRAGIC PREDICAMENT

So there he sat upon his precarious perch trying to reassume the posture which insured a good balance, clinging to the trunk with one hand and to the banana with the other.

And now that the encounter which had almost resulted in a tragic

sacrifice was over, and while our scout hero pauses triumphant, it may

be fitting to apologize to the reader for introducing our hero in the

act of eating. But indeed it was a question of introducing him in the

act of eating or of not introducing him at all.

For a story of Pee-wee Harris is necessarily more or less a story

of food. And this is a story abounding in cake and pie and waffles and

crullers and cookies and hot frankfurters. There will be found in it

also ice cream cones and jaw breakers and coconut bars and potatoes

roasted on sticks. Heroes of stories may have starved on desert islands

but there is to be none of that here.

In this tale, if you follow the adventures of our scout hero (who now at last appears before you as a star), you shall find lemonade side by side with first aid, and all the characters shall receive their just desserts, some of them (not to mention any names) two helpings.

So there he sat upon the branch, the mascot of the Raven Patrol, with an interior like the Mammoth Cave and a voice like the whisperings of the battle zone in France. Take a good look at him while he is quiet for ten seconds hand running. Everything about him is tremendous—except his size. He is built to withstand banter, ridicule and jollying; his sturdy nature is guaranteed proof against the battering assaults of unholy mirth from other scouts; his round face and curly hair are the delight of the girls of Bridgeboro; his loyalty is as the mighty rock of Gibraltar. A bully little scout he is—a sort of human Ford.

The question of removing the letter from the banana and getting rid of the banana (in the proper way) now presented itself to him. He took a bite of the banana and the letter almost fell. He then tried releasing his hold upon the trunk but that would not do. He then extracted the letter with his teeth which effectually prevented him from eating the banana.

What to do?

Steadying himself with one hand (he could not let go the trunk for so much as a moment), he brought the banana to his lips, held it between his teeth and took the letter in his unoccupied hand. As he bit into the banana the part remaining trembled and hung as on a thread; another moment and it would drop. The predicament was tragic. Slowly, but surely and steadily, the remainder of the banana broke away and fell—into the hand that held the letter.

Holding both letter and banana in the one perspiring palm, Pee-wee devoured first the one and then the other. Both were delicious, the letter particularly. It had one advantage over the banana, for he could only devour the banana once, whereas he devoured the contents of the letter several times. He wished that bananas and doughnuts were like letters.

CHAPTER III

AN INVITATION

The envelope was postmarked Everdoze which, with its one thousand two hundred and fifty—seven inhabitants, was the cosmopolitan center of Long Valley which ran (if anything in that neighborhood could be said to run) from Baxter City down below the vicinity of the bridge on the highway. That is, Long Valley bordered the highway on its western side for a distance of about ten miles. The valley was, roughly speaking, a couple of miles wide, very deep in places, and thickly wooded. It was altogether a very sequestered and romantic region. Through it, paralleling the highway, was a road, consisting mostly of two wagon ruts with a strip of grass and weeds between them. To traverse Long Valley one turned into this road where it left the highway at Baxters, and in the course of time the wayfarer would emerge out of this dim tract into the light of day where the unfrequented road came into the highway again below the bridge.

About midway of this lonely road was Everdoze, and in a pleasant old-fashioned white house in Everdoze lived Ebenezer Quig who once upon a time had married Pee-wee's Aunt Jamsiah. Pee-wee remembered his Aunt Jamsiah when she had come to make a visit in Bridgeboro and, though he had never seen her since, he had always borne her tenderly in mind because as a little (a very little) boy her name had always reminded him of jam. The letter, as has been said, bore the postmark of Everdoze and had been stamped by the very hand of Simeon Drowser, the local postmaster.

This is what the letter said:

DEAR WALTER:

        Your uncle has been pestering me to write
to you
        but Pepsy has been using the pen for her
school

                    exercise and I couldn't get hold of it
till today
                    when she went away with Wiggle, perch
fishing.
                    Licorice Stick says they're running in the
brook
                    most wonderful but you can't believe half
what he
                    says. Seems as if the perch know when
school closes,
                    least ways that's what your uncle says.

Pee-wee reread these enchanting words. Pepsy! Wiggle! Perch fishing!
Licorice Stick! And school closing! And perch that knew about it. That was the
sort of perch for Pee-wee. He read on:

                    I told your uncle I reckoned you wouldn't
care to
                    come here being you live in such a lively
place but he
                    said this summer you would like to come
for there will
                    be plenty for you to do because there is
going to be a
                    spelling match in the town hall and an
Uncle Tom's
                    Cabin show in August.

                    You can have plenty of milk and fresh eggs
and Miss
                    Arabella Bellison who has the school is
staying this
                    summer and she will let you in the
schoolhouse where
                    there is a library of more than forty
books but some of
                    the pages are gone Pepsy says.

                    She says to tell you she will show you
where she cut
                    her initials but I tell her not to put
such ideas in
                    your head and she knows how to climb in
even if the door

is locked, such goings on as she and Wiggle have, they
will be the death of me.

Well, Walter, you will be welcome if you can come
and spend the summer with us. I suppose you're a great
big boy by now; your mother was always tall for her age.
There are boys here who would like to be scout boys and
your uncle says you can teach them. We will do all we can
so that you have a pleasant summer if you come and tell
your mother we will be real glad to see you and will take
good care of you.

I can't write more now because I am putting up
preserves, one hundred jars already. The apples will be
rotting on the trees, it's a shame. You will think we are
very old-fashioned, I'm afraid.

Pee-wee paused and smacked his lips and nearly fell backward off the limb. One hundred jars of preserves and more coming, Apples rotting on the trees! All that remained to complete his happiness was a bush laden with ice cream cones growing wild. He read the concluding sentences:

Your uncle would be glad to go and bring you in the
buckboard but it would take very long and he is busy
haying so if you don't mind the bad road it would be
better for your father to send you in the automobile. Be
sure to turn off the highway to the right just above
Baxters. The road goes through the woods.

Your

loving

AUNT

JAMSIAH.

Steadying himself with one hand, Pee-wee took the letter between his teeth as if he were about to eat it. Then he cautiously let himself down so that he hung by his knees, then clutched the limb with his hands, hung for a moment with his legs dangling, and let go. In one sense he was upon earth but in another sense he was walking on air. ...

CHAPTER IV

HE GOES TO CONQUER

Thus it befell that on the second day after the receipt of this letter Pee-wee Harris was sitting beside Charlie, the chauffeur, in the fine sedan car belonging to Doctor Harris, advancing against poor, helpless Everdoze.

He traveled in all the martial splendor of his full scout regalia, his duffel bag stuffed to capacity with his aluminum cooking set and two extra scout suits. His diminutive but compact and sturdy little form was decorated with his scout jackknife hanging from his belt, his compass dangling from his neck, and his belt ax dragging down his belt in back.

A suggestive little dash of the culinary phase of scouting was to be seen in a small saucepan stuck in his belt like a deadly dagger. Thus if danger came he might confront his enemy with a sample of scout cookery and kill him on the spot.

His sleeves were bedecked with merit badges; from the end of his scout staff waved the flaunting emblem of the Raven Patrol; his stalking camera was swung over his shoulder like a knapsack; his nickel-plated scout whistle jangled against the saucepan and in his trousers pockets were a magnifying glass, three jaw breakers, a chocolate bar, a few inches of electric wiring, and a rubber balloon in a state of collapse.

The highway from Bridgeboro was a broad, smooth road, a temptation and a delight to speeders, where motorcycle cops lurked in the bushes hardly waiting for cars with New York licenses.

It was late in the afternoon when they reached Baxter City and here they turned into such a road as Charlie vowed he had never seen before.

Scarcely had they gone a mile over rocks and ruts when the dim woods closed in on either side, imparting a strange coolness. It was almost like going through a leafy tunnel projecting branches brushed the top of the car and mischievously grazed and tickled their faces. The voices of the birds, clear in the stillness, seemed to complain at this intrusion into their domain.

"I'd like to know how I'm going to get back through this jungle after dark," Charlie said. "I wonder what anybody wanted to start a village down here for?"

"Maybe—maybe they did it kind of absentmindedly," Pee-wee said. "I never started a village so I don't know."

"Well, you'll startle one anyway," Charlie said.

"I guess the village isn't much bigger than you are."

The road took them southward through the valley. They were not far west of the highway but the low country and the thick woods obscured it from view. They could hear the tooting of auto horns over that way and sometimes human voices sounding strange across the intervening solitude.

"I don't see why they didn't set the village down over at the highway; it's not more than a mile or so," Charlie said. "Maybe they were afraid the autos would run over it; safety first, hey? Nobody'll run over it here, that's one sure thing."

Pee-wee took the last bite of a hot frankfurter he had bought at a roadside shack on the highway and was now more free to talk.

"Listen," he said, "what's that?"

It was a distant rattling sound which began suddenly and ended suddenly. They both listened.

"There must be a bridge up there along the highway," Charlie said, "that's the sound of cars going over it. Loose planking, hey?"

Pee-wee listened to the rattling of the loose planks as another car sped over the unseen structure, little dreaming of the part that bridge was destined to play in his young life. The commonplace noise of the neglected flooring seemed emphasized by the quiet of the woodland. That reminder of human traffic, so near and yet so far and out of tune with all the gentler sounds of the valley, presented a strange contrast and jarred even Pee-wee's stout nerves.

"There goes another," Charlie said; "we must be nearer to the highway than I thought."

They had, indeed, inscribed a kind of loop and having passed its farthest point from the main road were traveling toward it again and would have emerged upon it just beyond the bridge but for the wood embowered and sequestered village which was their destination. The first sign of this village was a cow standing in the middle of the grass-grown road as if to challenge their approach. Perhaps she was stationed there as a sort of traffic cop.

CHAPTER V

ENTER PEPSY

It will be seen by a glance at the accompanying sketch that the village of Everdoze was about opposite the bridge on the highway. From this main road the village could be reached by a trail through the woods. On hearing of this, Charlie expressed regret that he had not allowed his passenger to make the final stage of the journey on foot.

"Well, I never in all my life !" said Aunt Jamsiah as Pee-wee stepped out of the car. "In goodness' name, where's the rest of you? I thought you were a great, tall, strapping boy. I hope your appetite's bigger than your body. And what on earth is that saucepan for? Are you going to cook us all alive? Did you ever see such a thing?" she added, speaking to Uncle Ebenezer who had stepped forward to welcome his nephew.

"He's all decked out like a carnival! He's just too killing!" She then proceeded to embrace him while his martial paraphernalia clanked and rattled.

"We won't need any more brass band," said a young girl in a gingham apron and with brick red hair in long tightly woven braids, who stood close by; "he's a melodeon. I don't see what they sent such a big car for with such a little boy. 'Taint no fit, it ain't."

Pee-wee gave this girl a withering look which she boldly returned, continuing to stare at him. Her face was covered with freckles and she was so unqualifiedly plain and homely in face and attire that she might be said to have been attractive on the ground of novelty.

"Pepsy," said Mrs. Quig, addressing her, "you shake hands with Walter and tell him you and he are going to be good friends. You come right here and do as I say now and no more of those looks."

"I ain't going to kiss him," the girl said by way of compromising.

"You give him a welcome just like Wiggle is doing," said Aunt Jamsiah, "and be ashamed that you have to learn your manners from such as he. You do as I say now."

"You're welcome—and I can beat you running," the girl said.

"Girls are afraid of snakes," Pee-wee retorted.

Meanwhile the individual who had been cited as a model of social correctness by Aunt Jamsiah stood upon the doorstep looking eagerly up into Pee-wee's face and wagging his tail with vigorous and lightning rapidity. Wiggle's tail was easily the fastest thing in Everdoze. His head vibrated in unison with it and his look of intentness carried with it all sorts of friendly expectations. He fairly shook with excitement and cordiality. He followed the sedan car a few yards upon its homeward journey and then, by a sudden impulse, deserted it and returned to a position directly in front of Pee-wee with wagging tail and questioning gaze. He seemed to say, "I'm ready for anything, the sky is the limit."

"You haven't had a bite to eat since breakfast and you're starving. I can tell it," said Aunt Jamsiah. "You come right in the kitchen."

"I had a lot of frankfurters and things at the places along the highway," Pee-wee said. "I had waffles at one place. I bet they make a lot of money along that road selling things. There are shacks all the way. All the autoists stop and buy things to eat. You can get tires and everything."

"Oh, I wouldn't want to eat tires," said Pepsy.

"You think you're smart, don't you?" Pee-wee said.

"What are your soldier clothes for?" the girl wanted to know.

"They're not soldier clothes," Pee-wee said;

"I'm a scout."

"I bet you don't know as much as Miss Bellson does."

"I bet I don't either," Pee-wee said, "so I win."

"She's the school teacher here and she knows everything."

"Did she know I was coming?"

"No she didn't and—"

"Then she doesn't know everything," Pee-wee said.

"Smarty, smarty!" the girl retorted, "I came out of an orphan home and that's more than you can say.".

"You only get one helping of dessert there," said Pee-wee. "I'd rather be a scout than an orphan. I know a feller who was an orphan and he was sorry for it afterwards."

"Are you going to stay all summer?"

"Till school opens," Pee-wee said.

"Do you want me to show you where there's a woodchuck hole?"

At this point Pee-wee was summoned again to the kitchen where he ate a sumptuous repast, after which Pepsy and Wiggle took him about and showed him the farm.

Pee-wee and Pepsy fenced a good deal but seemed to progress in this cautious and defensive way toward a friendly understanding. As for Wiggle, he danced about, following elusive scents that led nowhere, carried off and back again by quick impulse, till at last the three ended their tour of inspection at a little summer house which had been built over a spring by the roadside.

Here they drank of the bubbling, crystal water. Wiggle doing this as everything else, with erratic impulse, drinking a dozen times and not much at any time.

The dying sunlight painted the slopes of the valley with crimson tints and the countryside was very still. Through the woods to the west could be heard occasionally the discordant noise from the loose flooring of the bridge on the highway as an auto sped over it. In the quiet evening the sound, with its sudden start, its rattling clamor and its quick cessation, made a jarring note in all the surrounding peacefulness.

"That's what wakes me up in the morning, the mail wagon going over," Pepsy said; "I know it's time to get up then. Those planks can talk, they say the same thing every day."

```
You have to go back,
You have to go back,
You have to go back.
```

You listen to-morrow morning."

"They could never wake me up," Pee-wee said, which was probably true. "What do you mean about their saying you have to go back?"

"When Aunt Jamsiah took me, I was a probator. Do you know what that means?"

"It's what they do with people's wills," Pee-wee said.

"It means if I don't behave I have to go back to the orphan home," the girl said. "And every day I was afraid I'd have to go back—for a long, long time, I was. And when I was lying in bed mornings I'd hear the planks saying that—

```
You have to go back,
You have to go back.
```

just like that, and I'd get good and scared."

"You won't have to go back," said Pee-wee.

"You leave it to me, I'll fix it. Those planks—I've known lots of planks—and they can't tell the truth. Don't you care. I wouldn't believe what an old plank said. Trees are all right, but planks—"

"I don't notice it so much now," Pepsy said; "that was a year ago and Aunt Jamsiah says I'm all right and mind good except I'm a tomboy. That ain't so bad, is it? Being a tomboy? A girl and me tried to set the orphan home on fire because they licked us, but I'm good here. But I wish they'd put a new floor on that bridge. Anyway, Aunt Jamsiah says I'm good now."

Pee-wee was about to speak, but noticing that the girl's eyes were fixed upon a crimson patch on the hillside where the sun was going down, and seeing that her eyes sparkled strangely (for indeed they were not pretty eyes) he said nothing, like the bully little scout that he was.

"Anyway, one thing, I wouldn't let an old bridge get my goat, I wouldn't," he said finally, "and besides, you said you would show me a woodchuck hole."

CHAPTER VI

THE WAY OF THE SCOUT

Pepsy's right name was Penelope Pepperall and Aunt Jamsiah had taken her out of the County Home after the fire episode, by way of saving her from the worse influence of a reformatory. She and Uncle Ebenezer had agreed to be responsible for the girl, and Pepsy had spent a year of joyous freedom at the farm marred only by the threat hanging over her that she would be restored to the authorities upon the least suspicion of misconduct.

She had done her work faithfully and become a help and a comfort to her benefactors. She had a snappy temper and a sharp tongue and was, indeed, something of a tomboy. But Aunt Jamsiah, though often annoyed and sometimes chagrined, took a charitable view of these shortcomings and her generous heart was not likely to confound them with genuine misdoing.

So the stern condition of Pepsy's freedom had become something of a dead letter, except in her own fearful fancy, and particularly when that discordant voice of the bridge spoke ominously of her peril.

Pepsy had been trusted and had proven worthy of the trust. She had never known any mother or father, nor any home save the institution from which Aunt Jamsiah had rescued her, and she had grown to love her kindly guardians and the old farm where she had much work but also much freedom. "Chores will keep her out of mischief," Aunt Jamsiah had said.

Wiggle's ancestry and social standing were quite as much a mystery as Pepsy's; he was not an aristocrat, that is certain, and having no particular chores to do was free to devote his undivided time to mischief; he concentrated on it, as the saying is, and thereby accomplished wonders. He was Pepsy's steady comrade and the partner of all her adventurous escapades.

Pepsy was not romantic and imaginative, her freckled face and tightly braided red hair and thin legs with wrinkled cotton stockings, protested against that. She had a simple mind with a touch of superstition. It was a kind of morbid dread of the institution she had left which had conjured that ramshackle old bridge up on the highway into an ominous voice of warning, She hated the bridge and dreaded it as a thing haunted.

Pee-wee soon became close friends with these two, and from a rather cautious and defensive beginning Pepsy soon fell victim to the spell of the little scout, as indeed everyone else did. Pepsy did not surrender without a struggle. She showed Pee-wee the woodchuck hole and Pee-wee, after a minute's skillful search, showed her the other hole, or back entrance, under a stone wall.

"There are always two," he told her, "and one of them is usually under a stone wall. They're smart, woodchucks are."

"Are they as smart as you?" she wanted to know.

"Smarter," Pee-wee admitted, generously; "they're smarter than skunks and even skunks are smarter than I am."

"I like you better than skunks," she said. Wiggle seemed to be of the same opinion. "I like all the scouts on account of you," she said.

No one could be long in Pee-wee's company without hearing about the scouts; he was a walking (or rather a running and jumping) advertisement of the organization. He told Pepsy about tracking and stalking and signaling and the miracles of cookery which his friend Roy Blakeley had performed.

"Can he cook better than you?" Pepsy wanted to know, a bit dubiously.

"Yes, but I can eat more than he can," Pee-wee said. And that seemed to relieve her.

"I can make a locust come to me," he added, and suiting the action to the word he emitted a buzzing sound which brought a poor deluded locust to his very hand. At such wonder-working she could only gape and stare. Wiggle appeared to claim the locust as a souvenir of the scout's magic.

"You let it go, Wiggle," Pee-wee said. "If you want to be a scout you can't kill anything that doesn't do any harm. But you can kill snakes and mosquitoes if you want to." Evidently it was the dream of Wiggle's life to be a scout for he released the locust to Pee-wee, wagging his tail frantically.

"You have to be loyal, too," the young propagandist said; "that's a rule. You have to be helpful and think up ways to help people. No matter what happens you have to be loyal."

"Do you have to be loyal to orphan homes?" Pepsy wanted to know. "If they lick you do you have to be loyal to them?"

Here was a poser for the scout. But being small Pee-wee was able to wriggle out of almost anything. "You have to be loyal where loyalty is due," he said. "That's what the rule says; it's Rule Two. But, anyway, there's another rule and that's Rule Seven and it says you have to be kind. You can't be kind licking people, that's one sure thing. So it's a technicality that you don't have to be loyal to an orphan home. You can ask any lawyer because that's what you call logic."

"Deadwood Gamely's father is a lawyer," Pepsy said, "and I hate Deadwood Gamely and I wouldn't go to his house to ask his father. He's a smarty and I hit him with a tomato. Have I got a right to do that—if he's a smarty?"

Here was another legal technicality, but Pee-wee was equal to the occasion. "A—a scout has to be a—he has to have a good aim," he said.

CHAPTER VII

A BIG IDEA

They had been driving the cows home during this learned exposition on scouting. Two things were now perfectly clear to Pepsy's simple mind. One, that she would be loyal at any cost, loyal to her new friend, and through him to all the scouts. She knew them only through him. They were a race of wonder-workers away off in the surging metropolis of Bridgeboro. She could not aspire to be one of them, but she could be loyal, she could "stick up" for them.

The other matter which was now settled, once and for all, was that it was all right to throw a tomato at a person you hated provided only that you hit the mark. Aunt Jamsiah had been all wrong in her anger at that exploit which had stirred the village. For to throw a tomato at the son of Lawyer Gamely was aiming very high.

The son of Lawyer Gamely had a Ford and worked in the bank at Baxter City and was a mighty sport who wore white collars and red ties and said that "Everdoze was asleep and didn't have brains enough to lie down," and all such stuff.

Pee-wee let down the bars while the patient cows waited, and Scout Wiggle (knowing that a scout should be helpful) gave the last cow a snip on the leg to help her along.

Here, at these rustic bars, ended Pepsy's chores for the day and in the delightful interval before supper she and Pee-wee lolled in the well house by the roadside. Wiggle, with characteristic indecision, chased the cows a few yards, returned to his companions, darted off to chase the cows again, deserted that pastime with erratic suddenness, and returned again wagging his tail and looking up intently as if to ask, "What next?" Then he lay down panting. Mr. Ellsworth, Pee-wee's scoutmaster, would have said that Wiggle lacked method. ...

"If I had a lot of money," Pepsy said, "you could teach me all the things that scouts know and I'd pay you ever so much. Once I had forty cents but I spent it at the Mammoth Carnival. I paid ten cents to throw six balls so I could get a funny doll and I never hit the doll and when I only had ten cents left I made believe the doll was Deadwood Gamely and I hated and hated with all my might while I threw the ball the last six times but I couldn't hit the doll."

"You can't aim so good when you're mad," Pee-wee said, "so if you want to hit somebody with a tomato or an egg or anything like that you just have kind thoughts about the person that you're aiming at, only you're not supposed to throw tomatoes and eggs and things because you can have more fun eating them. I wouldn't waste a tomato on that feller because anyway you've got your tongue."

"You can't sass him," said Pepsy, "because he uses big words and he's such a smarty and he makes you feel silly and then you begin to cry and get mad. When he says I'm an orphan and things—and things—Wiggle hates him, too, don't you, Wiggle?" The girl was almost crying then and Pee-wee comforted her.

"Do you think I don't know any long words?" he said. "I know some of the longest words that were ever invented and—and—even I can make special ones myself. Once I—don't you cry—once I was kept in school and Julia Carson was kept in too, because she wriggled in her seat—you know how girls do. I had to choose a word and write it a hundred times and I didn't want to get through too soon, because I wanted to get out the same time she did. So I chose the word incomprehensibility, and I—"

"Is that girl pretty?" Pepsy wanted to know.

"She's got a wart on her finger. It's the best one I ever saw," Pee-wee said. "She's afraid to get in a boat, that girl is."

"I hate her," Pepsy said.

"What for?" Pee-wee inquired. "Because she has a wart? Don't you know it's good luck to have warts?"

"Because—because she was bad and had to stay after school," Pepsy said.

"That shows how much you know about logic," Pee-wee said, "because I had to stay too and I was worse than she was. So there."

"I wouldn't be afraid to get in a boat," Pepsy said proudly.

"I never said she was like you," Pee-wee declared. "She's not a tomboy."

Pepsy seemed comforted.

"You leave that feller to me," Pee-wee said. "I can handle Roy Blakeley and all his patrol and they're a lot of jolliers—they think they're so smart."

"I like you better than all of them," Pepsy said. "Sometimes I'm kept after school too, you can ask Miss Bellison."

"One thing sure, I like you well enough to be partners with you," Pee-wee said. "Do you want me to tell you something? I thought of a way to make a lot of money, and if I do I'm going to buy three new tents for our troop. Do you want to go partners with me? We'll say the tents are from both of us and we'll have a lot of fun."

"I had a dollar once and I sent it to the heathens," Pepsy said, "and I'd rather help you than the heathens, because I like you better."

"Heathens are all right," Pee-wee said, "and I'm not saying anything against heathens, especially wild ones, but we're just as wild. You ought to go to Temple Camp and see how wild we are."

He did not look very wild as he sat upon the narrow seat with his knees drawn up and his scout hat on the back of his head showing his curly hair.

The girl gazed at his natty khaki attire, the row of merit badges on his sleeve, the trophies of his heroic triumphs. She was not the first to feel the lure of a uniform. But it was the first uniform she had ever seen at close range, for in the wartime she had been in that frowning brick structure which still haunted her.

"I'll help you because you can do everything and you know a lot," she said.

In the fullness of her generosity and loyalty to Pee-wee's prowess she never reminded him or even thought of the things she could do which he could not. She would not do her little optional chore of milking a cow for fear he might perceive her superiority in this little item of proficiency. Poor girl, she was a better scout than she knew.

"If you think it up I'll do all the work, and then we'll be even," she said.

So Pee-wee told her of the colossal scheme which his lively imagination had conceived.

"It all started with a hot frankfurter," he said. "If I hadn't bought a hot frankfurter I wouldn't have thought of it. So that shows you how important a frankfurter is—kind of. Maybe a person might get to be a millionaire just starting with a frankfurter, you never can tell. ..."

CHAPTER VIII

MAKING PLANS

"I bought that frankfurter at a shack up on the highway and while I was eating it I just happened to think that as long as there's lots of fruit and things here and as long as you know how to make fudge, we'd start a shack right here in this well house and sell lemonade and fruit and fudge and cookies and things, and if we make lots of money I'd go up to Baxter City and buy some auto accessories like spark plugs and tire tape and things and we'd sell those, too. We'd put signs on the trees along the road telling people to stop here and I know how to make up signs so as to get people good and hungry. You have them say that things are hot in the pan and you have to have drinks with names like arctic and all like that. I know how to make them hungry and thirsty and I've got a balloon that I can blow up—see? And we'd print something on it and tie it to Wiggle's tail and make him walk up and down the road. What do you say? Isn't it a peachy scheme? Will you help me?"

No dream of Pee-wee's could be impossible of fulfillment. With him, to try was to succeed, according to Pepsy's simple and unbounded faith. The plan must be all right, and wondrous in its possibilities. It was all inspiration—born of a frankfurter. It was not for poor Pepsy to take issue with this master mind.

Yet she did venture to say, "Not very many autos come down here, only a few that go through to Berryville. Licorice Stick—"

"That's a dandy name," Pee-wee said.

"He goes by a dozen times a day, but he hasn't got any money, and Mr. Flint goes by but he's a miser and Doctor Killem goes by in his buggy and he says people eat too much—"

"He's crazy!" Pee-wee shouted.

"And that's everybody that goes by except a few when they have the town fair in Berryville."

For a moment Pee-wee paused, balked but not beaten. "There's going to be an Uncle Tom's Cabin show in Berryville," he said, "and the town fair, that's two things. Let's start in and maybe later there'll be some summer boarders in Berryville. We'll have waffles—I can make those. And we'll have lemonade and fruit and all kinds of things and when you're doing your chores I'll tend counter. We'll make a lot of money, you see if we don't."

In her generous confidence, Pepsy was quite carried away by Pee-wee's enthusiasm. She knew (who better than she?) that strangers never came along that lonely by-road. But she believed that somehow they would come when the scout waved his magic wand.

"And I'll make cookies," she said, "and all the things to eat and you can print the signs—"

"And shout to the people going by," Pee-wee concluded enthusiastically. "You have to yell ALL HOT! THEY'RE ALL HOT! Just like that."

Few could resist this, Pepsy least of all. "Let's go and ask Aunt Jamsiah about it right now," she said.

"Let me do it, I know how to handle her," said Pee-wee.

And Pepsy deferred to the master mind, as usual.

CHAPTER IX

IT PAYS TO ADVERTISE

Permission to use the well house once secured, preparations for the vast enterprise progressed rapidly. The very next day, while Pepsy was at her chores, Pee-wee built a counter in the shack and sitting at this he printed signs to be displayed along the woody approaches to this mouth-watering dispensary.

Neither the gloomy predictions of his uncle nor the laughing skepticism of his aunt dimmed his enterprising ardor. The signs which he printed with his uncle's crate stencil, procured from the barn, bespoke the variety of tempting offerings which existed so far only in his fertile mind.

He was somewhat handicapped in the preparation of these signs by the largeness of the perforated letters of the stencil and the limited size of the cards. He had preferred cards to paper because they would not blow and tear and Aunt Jamsiah had given him a pile of these, uniform in size, on one side of which had been printed election notices of the previous year. It was impossible, therefore, for Pee-wee to include all of each tempting announcement on one card, so he used two cards for each reminder to the public. Thus on one card he printed FRANKFURTERS and on its mate intended for posting just below, the palate-tickling conclusion, SIZZLING HOT.

```
FRANKFURTERS
SIZZLING HOT  —>
```

This is how the sign would appear upon some fence or tree. It would be a knockout blow to any hungry wayfarer.

Another two—card sign, intended for warmer weather, read:

```
ICE CREAM
<—  COLD AND COOLING
```

Other signs originating in Pee-wee's fertile mind and covering the range of food and drink and auto accessories were these:

```
PEANUT TAFFY
SWEET AND DELICIOUS  —>


OUR TIRE TAPE
<—  STICKS LIKE GLUE
```

```
           NON SKID
          CHAINS -->


           FRESH
        <-- BANANAS


           DRINK
        SWEET CIDER -->


           MAGIC
      <-- CARBON REMOVER
```

There were many others, enough to decorate the road for miles in both directions. If Pepsy as chef could live up to Pee-wee's promises the neighborhood would soon become famous. That was her one forlorn hope, that the fame of their offerings would get abroad and lure the traffic from its wonted path. But Pee-wee's enthusiasm and energy carried all before them like a storming column and she was soon as hopeful and confident as he.

When her chores were finished that afternoon she hurried to their refreshment parlor, where Pee-wee sat behind the new counter like a stern schoolmaster, cards strewn about him, his round face black with stencil ink, still turning out advertising bait for the public.

"I don't care what they say," she panted; "we're going to make a lot of money and buy the tents. I tripped on the third step in the house just now and that means surely we'll have good luck and I can help just as much as if I was a really truly scout, can't I? Aunt Jamsiah says if I make a lot of doughnuts you'll just eat them all and there won't be any to sell. We mustn't eat the things ourselves, must we?"

"That shows how much she knows," Pee-wee said; "we might have to do that to make the people hungry. If they see me eating a doughnut and looking very happy, won't that make them want to buy some? We have upkeep expenses, don't we?"

"Yes, and I'm sorry I didn't tell her that," Pepsy said, "but I never thought of it. You always think of things. I'm going to wash the ink off your face, so hold still."

She dipped her gingham apron under the trapdoor in the flooring where the clear, cool water was, and taking his chin in her coarse little freckly hands, washed the face of her hero and partner. And meanwhile Wiggle tugged on her apron as if he thought she were inflicting some injury upon the boy.

So blinded was Pee-wee by this vigorous bath and so preoccupied the others that for the moment none of them noticed the young fellow of about twenty who, with hat tilted rakishly on the side of his head and cigarette drooping from the corner of his mouth, stood in the road watching them.

CHAPTER X

DEADWOOD GAMELY TALKS BUSINESS

Deadwood Gamely was the village sport and enjoyed a certain prestige because his father was a lawyer. He was also somewhat of an object of awe because he went to Baxter City every day, and worked in the bank there.

His ramshackle Ford roadster was considered an evidence of the terribly reckless extravagance of his habits, but it was really nothing more than a sort of pocketbook, since all his money went into it, and a very shabby one at that. He had a cheap wit and swaggeringly condescending air which he practiced on the simple inhabitants of Everdoze, and in his banter he was not always kind. Yet notwithstanding that he was tawdry both in dress and speech the villagers did not venture much into the conversational arena with him because they knew that they were not his equals in banter and retort.

"Hello, little orphan Annie," he said. "Bungel was telling me the wagon is coming for you pretty soon. Over the hill to the poorhouse. Ever hear that song? What's that you've got there, a soldier? Watcher doing with him? Lucky kid, I'd like to be a soldier."

"What were you, a slacker?" Pee-wee shouted.

This was not the kind of retort that Deadwood Gamely was accustomed to hearing and he gave a quick look at the small stranger in khaki who sat behind the counter like a judge on the bench staring straight at him.

"Don't get him riled," Pepsy whispered. "He likes to get me riled so's just to make me feel silly; it's—it's Deadwood Gamely. He's always togged out swell like that," she added fearfully.

"The only thing that's swell about him is his head," said Pee-wee in his loudest voice. "Don't you be scared of him, I'm here."

"What's that?" said the young man in a tone intended to be darkly menacing.

"You'd better put your hat on the top of your head or it'll blow off," said Pee-wee. "I said that I'm here. Let's hear you deny it. If I was a crow I might be afraid of you."

Slightly taken aback by his ready retorts, the young man could only say, "If you were a crow, hey?" He stepped a little closer to the counter but the ominous advance did not alarm Pee-wee in the least. He sat behind his card-strewn counter holding the stencil brush like a sort of weapon ready to besmear that face of sneering assurance if its owner ventured too near.

"So I'm a scarecrow, eh?" Mr. Gamely said with a side glance at Pepsy. He was not going to have her witness his discomfiture at the hands of this glib little stranger. Moreover, a slur at his personal splendor was a very grave matter and not to be overlooked.

"I don't like fresh kids," said Mr. Deadwood Gamely, advancing with an air of veiled menace.

"Sometimes they get so fresh they have to be salted a little. Don't you think you'd better take that back?"

Pepsy waited, fearful, breathless.

"Sure I will," said Pee-wee; "the next scarecrow I meet I'll apologize to him."

Deadwood Gamely paused. His usual procedure in an affair of this kind would have been to advance quickly, ruffle his victim's hair in a goading kind of swaggerish good humor and send him sprawling. He would not really have hurt a youngster like Pee-wee but he would have made him look and feel ridiculous.

But a glance at Pee-wee's gummy stencil brush reminded Mr. Gamely that discretion was the better part of valor. A dexterous dab or two of that would have put an end to all his glory. Pee-wee left no doubt about this.

"This summer-house is on private land," he said, "and I'm the boss of it. If you try to get fresh with me I'll paint you blacker—blacker than a—than a tomato could—I will. You come ten steps nearer, I dare you to."

Gamely paused irresolute, at which Pepsy, under protection of her partner's terrible threat, set up a provoking laugh. Wiggle, appearing to sense the situation, began to bark up-roariously. There was nothing for the baffled village sport to do but retreat as gracefully as he could.

"Can't you take a joke?" he said weakly. "Do you think I'd hurt you?"

"I know you wouldn't," said Pee-wee; "you wouldn't get the chance. You think you're smart, don't you, talking about the wagon coming to get her and getting her all scared."

Deadwood Gamely broke into a very excessive but false laugh. "No harm intended," he said, vaulting on to the fence and sitting discreetly at that distance. "What's all this going on here? Going to have a circus or play store or something?"

Pee-wee was always magnanimous in victory. Abiding enmity was a thing he knew not. So now he laid down his stencil brush (within easy reach) and said, "We're going to start a refreshment shack and sell fruit and lemonade and waffles and things and maybe auto accessories and souvenirs."

Pepsy seemed a bit uncomfortable as Pee-wee said this, perhaps just a trifle ashamed. She was afraid that this clever, sophisticated young fellow would ridicule their enterprise, as indeed there was good reason to do. Yet she felt ashamed, too, of her momentary faithlessness to Pee-wee.

"Maybe some people will pass here when they have the carnival at Berryville," she said, half apologetically.

To her surprise Deadwood Gamely, instead of emitting an uproarious, mocking laugh, appeared to be thinking.

"Bully for you," he finally said, looking all about as if to size up the surroundings. "Right on the job, hey? I'd like to buy some stock in that enterprise. Whose idea is it? Yours, kiddo?"

"We're going to make money enough to buy three tents for the scout troop I belong to," Pee-wee said.

"Visiting here, hey?"

"I live in Bridgeboro, New Jersey; I'm here for the summer."

Deadwood Gamely sat on the fence still looking, about him and whistling. Then, instead of bursting forth in derisive merriment as Pepsy dreaded he would do, he made an astonishing remark.

"I tell you what I'll do," he said. "You kids take care of the place and furnish the fruit and stuff and I'll put up the coin for all the stuff you have to buy— chewing gum, and accessories, and souvenirs and junk that has to be got in the city, and we'll share even. I'll put up the capital and be a silent partner. How does that strike you? You two will be the active partners. We'll make the thing go big. I mean what I say."

"What's a silent partner?" Pee-wee demanded.

"Oh, that's just the fellow that puts up the money and keeps in the background sort of, and nobody knows he's interested."

"I'd rather be a noisy partner," Pee-wee said.

"I wouldn't be silent for anybody, I wouldn't't." Deadwood Gamely paused a moment, smiling.

"No, but you could keep a secret, couldn't you?" he asked.

CHAPTER XI

TWO IS A COMPANY—THREE IS BAD LUCK

Pee-wee and Pepsy were not agreed about allowing this third person to buy into their enterprise. Pepsy was suspicious because she could not understand it. But Pee-wee, quick to forget dislikes and trifling injuries, was strong for the new partner.

"He's all right," he told her, "and scouts are supposed to be kind and help people and maybe he wants to reform and we ought to help him get into business."

"He's a smarty and I hate him and three is bad luck," was all that Pepsy

could say. Then she broke down crying, "Miss
Bellison hates him, too,"
  she sobbed, "and—and if people sit three in a seat
in a wagon one
  of them dies inside of a year. Now you go and spoil
it all by having
  three."

  "You get three jaw breakers for a cent," Pee-wee
said. "Lots of times
  I bought them three for a cent, and I bought peanut
bars three for a
  cent too, and I never died inside of a year, you can
ask anybody."

"I don't care, I want to have it all alone with you," she sobbed.

"If we count Wiggle in that will make four," Pee-wee said, "and none of us
will die. If the customers die that doesn't count, does it?"

Pepsy did not hear this rather ominous prediction about those who would eat
the waffles and the taffy. Her hate and her tears were her only arguments, but
they won the day.

"He's got a Ford," Pee-wee said in scornful final plea, "and he can put up
money enough for us to buy lots of sundries and pretty soon we'll have money
enough to start other refreshment places and he can be the one to ride around
he'll be kind of field manager. It shows how much girls know about business,"
he added disgustedly. "I bet you don't even know what capital means."

"It means what you begin a sentence with," Pepsy sobbed.

"You don't want it to be a success," he charged scornfully.

"You're a mean thing to say that," she sobbed, "and I do—I do—I do want it to
be a success—and—and—even if it isn't we'll have lots of fun if it's just us two.
Because anyway we can make believe, and that's fun."

"What do you mean, make believe?" Pee-wee demanded. "Aren't we going to
make enough to buy the tents? That shows how much you know about scouts. If
scouts make up their minds to do things they do them—and they don't make
believe. I'll give in to you about that feller but you have to say we're not going to
just make believe and play store, because that's the way girls do. You have to
say you're in earnest and cross your heart and say we'll make a lot of money—
sure."

Pepsy just sobbed. Her staunch little heart (when she would listen to it) told
her how forlorn was the hope of "really and truly" success along that by-road
through the wilderness. But the imagination which could be terrified by the
rattle of that planking on the old bridge was quite equal to finding satisfaction in
"playing store" and in seeing customers where there were none. Pee-wee
believed that anything could be done by power of will. She would find the

utmost joy in pretending. No, not the utmost joy, for the utmost joy would be to buy the tents. ...

"You have to say we're not pretending like girls do" he insisted relentlessly as she buried her head in her poor little thin arm and sobbed more and more. "You have to say it. Do you cross your heart? Is it going to be a success? Are we going to make lots of money—sure? You have to say we're not just fooling like girls. Do you say it? You're not just playing?"

"N—no."

"Cross your heart."

Her freckly hands went crossways on her heaving breast.

"It's business just like—like Mr. Drowser's store. Is it?"

She nodded her head.

"Say If I cross my heart and don't mean what I say, I hope to drop dead the very same day. Say that?"

So she sobbed out those terrible words. "And you promise not to let him come in?" she added, provisionally.

He promised and then suddenly she raised her head with a kind of jerk, as if possessed by a sudden, new spirit of determination. Her eyes were streaming. She looked straight into his face. There was fire enough in her eyes to dry the tears.

"If—if you wish a thing you—you get—you get it," she gulped. "Because I wished and wished to go away from that—that place—and now I made up my mind that we're going to—going to—make a lot of money for—for you—I just did."

She did not say how they were going to do it.

CHAPTER XII

THE ADVERTISING DEPARTMENT

The next morning Pee-wee strode forth and made the magnanimous sacrifice heroically. He found Deadwood Gamely in front of Simeon Drowser's village store, talking with two men who sat in an auto.

The auto was so large and handsome that it looked out of place in front of Simeon Drowser's store, and the men who occupied it looked like city men. It encouraged Pee-wee (or rather confirmed his assurance of success) to see this sumptuous car in Everdoze, for it proved that people did come to that sequestered village. He pictured these two prosperous looking business men with frankfurters in their hands, their mouths dripping with mustard.

Pee-wee was nothing if not self-possessed, his scout uniform was his protection, and he strode up and spoke quite to the point to the young fellow who leaned against the car with one foot on the running board.

"We decided not to take you in as a partner," he said, "because we want to have it all to ourselves and I came to tell you."

Deadwood Gamely seemed rather taken aback, but whether it was because of this refusal of his offer, or because Pee-wee's loud announcement embarrassed him before the strangers it would be hard to say. Seeing that the diminutive scout no longer held the deadly stencil brush he removed Pee-wee's hat with a swaggering good humor, ruffled his hair, and said (rather disconcertedly), "All right, kiddo; so long."

Pee-wee had anticipated an argument with Gamely and he was surprised at the promptness and agreeableness of his dismissal. Two things, one seen and one heard, remained in his memory as he trudged back to the farm. One was a brief case lying on the back seat of the auto on which was printed WALLACE CONSTRUCTION CO. The other was something he heard one of the men say after he had returned a little way along the road.

"I didn't think you were such a fool," the man said, evidently to young Gamely. Within a few seconds more the auto was rolling away.

It seemed to Pee-wee that Gamely had told the men of his proposal to join the big enterprise and that they had denounced his wisdom and judgment.

But Pee-wee was not the one to be discouraged by that. "Maybe they know all about construction," he said to himself, "but that's not saying they know all about refreshment shacks. I bet they don't know any more about eats than I do." Which in all probability was the case.

On the way back to the farm, Pee-wee noticed in a field the most outlandish scarecrow he had ever seen. It was sitting on a stone wall, and it must have been a brave crow that would have ventured within a mile of that ridiculous bundle of rags. The face was effectually concealed by a huge hat as is the case with most scarecrows, and all the cast-off clothing of Everdoze for centuries back seemed combined here in incongruous array.

What was Pee-wee's consternation when he beheld this figure actually descend from the fence and come shambling over toward him. If the legs were not on stilts they were certainly the longest legs he had ever seen, and they must have been suspended by a kind of universal joint for they moved in every direction while bringing their burden forward.

Upon this absurd being's closer approach, Pee-wee perceived it to be a negro as thin and tall as a clothes pole, and so black that the blackness of sin would seem white by comparison and the arctic night like the blazing rays of midsummer. This was Licorice Stick whose home was nowhere in particular, whose profession was everything and chiefly nothing.

"I done seed yer comin'," he said with a smile a mile long which shone in the surrounding darkness like the midnight sun of Norway. His teeth were as conspicuous as tombstones, and on close inspection Pee-wee saw that his tattered regalia was held together by a system of safety pins placed at strategic points. The terrible responsibility of suspenders was borne by a single strand consisting of a key ring chain connected with a shoe lace and this ran through a harness pin which, if the worst came to the worst, would act as a sort of emergency stop. Licorice Stick was built in the shape of a right angle, his feet being almost as long as his body and they flapped down like carpet beaters when he walked.

"You stayin' wib Uncle Eb?" he asked. "I seed yer yes' day. I done hear yer start a sto."

"A what?" Pee-wee asked, as they walked along together.

"A sto— you sell eats, hey?"

"Oh, you mean a store," Pee-wee said.

"I help you," said the lanky stranger; "me'n Pepsy, we good friends. She hab to go back to dat workhouse, de bridge it say so. Dat bridge am a sperrit."

"You're crazy," Pee-wee said. "What's the use of being scared at an old rattly bridge. If you want to help us I'll tell you how you can do it. I made a lot of signs and you can tack them all up on the trees along the road for us if you want to. I'll show you just how to do it."

No one was at the shack when they reached it for Pepsy was about her household duties, so she had no knowledge of this new recruit in their enterprise. Pee-wee's conscience was clear in this matter, however, for he had enlisted Licorice Stick as an employee, at the staggering salary of twenty-five cents a week; there was no thought of his being a partner. The willing assistance of his new friend would leave his own time free for more important duties, and the advertising work once done, Licorice Stick was to devote his time to catching fish for the "sto" and other incidental duties.

Pee-wee now arranged his advertising masterpieces in order for posting. The imposing type on the cards impressed Licorice Stick deeply. He could not read two words but he seemed to sense the sensational announcements, and the arrow which Pee-wee had made on each card to indicate the direction of the shack was regarded by him as a sort of mystic symbol.

"This is the way you have to do," Pee-wee said; "now pay attention, because it pays to advertise. There are two cards for each sign, see?"

"Dey's nice black print," Licorice Stick said with reverent appreciation. "En dey's de magic sign, too."

"That tells them where the place is," Pee-wee said. "Now, you keep the cards just the way I give them to you and always tack them up with the arrow pointing this way see? Here's a hammer and here's some tacks. When you come to a nice big tree or a wooden fence or an old barn, you're supposed to tack them up; and be sure to do it the way I tell you. Now, suppose you're going to tack up the first card—the one on the top of the pile. You tack it up and right close under it you tack up the next one, and it will say:"

FRANKFURTERS

SIZZLING HOT —>

"Mmm—mm!" exclaimed Licorice Stick, as if a hot frankfurter had actually been produced by this ingenious card trick.

"Then you go along a little way," said Pee-wee, "till you come to another good place, maybe a fence or something, and you tack up the next one and right underneath it you tack up the next one; always take the next one off the top of the pile, see."

ICE CREAM

<— COLD AND COOLING

Pee-wee repeated, holding the next two cards up. This palate tickling sleight-of-hand seemed like a miracle to the smiling, astonished messenger. Pee-wee seemed a kind of magician summoning up luscious concoctions with a magic wand. The fifth and sixth cards were held together for a moment and lo, Licorice Stick listened to the mouth-watering announcement that peanut taffy was sweet and delicious.

No "sperrit" of Licorice Stick's acquaintance had ever cast a spell like this. They had called in weird voices but they had never contrived a menu before his very eyes.

He went forth armed with the hammer and tacks and a pile of mysterious cards, a little proud but trembling a little, too. There was something uncanny about this; he would see it through but it was a strange, dark business. He shuffled along the road, peering fearfully into the woods now and again when suddenly a terrible apparition appeared before him. He stood stark still, his eyes bulging out of his head, his hands shaking and cold with fear. ...

CHAPTER XIII

PEPSY'S SECRET

"Sally Knapp says we ought to have some barrels to put the money in," said Pepsy as they were decorating their little wayside booth on the day of the grand opening. "I don't care what she says."

She was feeling encouraged, and cheerful for indeed the little summer-house looked gay and attractive in its bunting drapery and flaunting pennants. Failure could not lurk in such festal array, the tin dishpan full of greasy doughnuts, the homemade rolls and fresh sausages (which were better than any common wayside frankfurters) would certainly lure the hungry thither. The world would seek these things out. And were not the people of the grand carnival at Berryville to pass here that very day, followed, no doubt, by gay pleasure seekers?

To be sure there were no auto accessories yet, for there was no capital, but there was lemonade and candy and cider and homemade ice cream and there

30

was Scout Harris wearing a kitchen apron ten times too big for him, tied with a wonderful, spreading bow in back, and a paper hat spotlessly white.

The advertising department had not reported but no doubt the woods were calling to the wayfarers in glaring red and black, or would as soon as the wayfarers put in an appearance. Pepsy wore her Sunday gingham dress embellished with a sash of patriotic bunting.

"Don't you care what the girls say," Pee-wee advised her as he sat on the counter eating a piece of peanut taffy by way of testing the stock, so that he might the more honestly recommend it. "I wouldn't let any girls jolly me, I wouldn't. Lots of girls tried to jolly me but they never got away with it."

"Did that girl that was kept after school try to jolly you?" Pepsy asked.

"I wouldn't let any girls jolly me," Pee-wee said, ignoring the specific question and speaking with difficulty, because of the stickiness of the taffy. "They think they're smart, girls do; I don't mean you, but most of them. I know how to handle them all right. They try to make a fool of you and then just giggle, but the last laugh is the best, that's one sure thing."

"I told her she was a freshy," Pepsy said, "and that she wouldn't dare talk like that in front of you because you'd make a fool of her."

"I should worry about girls," Pee-wee said.

"I'm not worrying about our refreshment shack anyway," Pepsy said, "because now I know it will be lots and lots of a success. And maybe you can buy four or five tents and lots of other things. Every night in bed I keep saying:

```
It has to succeed,
It has to succeed,
```

and I make believe the floor on the bridge says that instead. But sometimes it says I have to go back. When the wind blows this way I can hear it loud. I know a secret that I thought of all by myself; I thought about it when I was lying in bed listening. And I can make us get lots of money, I can make it, oh, lots and lots and lots of a success. So I don't care any more what people say. I told Aunt Jamsiah I knew a secret and I could make us get lots of money here and she said I should tell her and I wouldn't."

"Till you tell me?" Pee-wee asked.

"No, I wouldn't tell anybody."

"You ought to tell me because we're partners." "I wouldn't tell anybody," she said, shaking her head emphatically so that her red braids lashed about; "not even if you gave me—as much as a dollar. ..."

CHAPTER XIV

SUSPENSE

Soon the gorgeous chariot containing the carnival paraphernalia came lumbering along en route for Berryville. It was a vision of red and gold with wheels that looked like pinwheels in a fireworks display.

The one discordant note about it was the rather startling projection of the heads and legs of animals here and there as if the wagon were returning from a hunt in South Africa. But these were only the disconnected parts of a merry-go-round.

Upon the white and silver wind organ which arose out of this ghastly display sat a personage in cap and bells with face elaborately decorated in every color of the rainbow. He was distributing printed announcements to the gaping citizens of Everdoze. Not so much as a frankfurter or a glass of lemonade did the people of this motley caravan buy.

It was late in the afternoon and Pee-wee and Pepsy were feeling the tedium of waiting when suddenly the sound of merry laughter burst upon, their ears and somebody said, "Oh, I think it's perfectly adorable to be on the wrong road! I just adore being lost! And I never saw anything so perfectly excruciating in my life!"

"It's an auto full of girls," said Pee-wee, adjusting his paper hat upon his head; "they come from the city, I can tell; you leave them to me."

"I never saw anything so adorably funny in all my life," the partners now heard. "I just have a headache from laughing."

"I know that kind," said Pee-wee; "they've got the giggles. You leave them to me."

Pepsy was ready enough to defer to the master mind, the more so because this approach of their first probable customers gave her a kind of stage fright. She was seized with sudden terror and the dishpan full of doughnuts shook in her hands as she placed it in full view by Pee-wee's order.

The auto was evidently picking its way along the hubbly road in second gear. "We'll find a place where we can turn around somewhere," said a man's voice good humoredly.

"Not till we've gorged ourselves with food," the voice of a girl caroled forth.

Pee-wee gave his white paper cap a final adjustment, stood the pan of taffy enticingly in full view and waited as a pugilist waits, for the adversary's next move.

"I am going to have a saucerful of ground glass, the latest breakfast food," a female voice sang merrily. At which there was a chorus of laughter.

"What did she say?" Pepsy asked.

"Girls are crazy," Pee-wee said.

Pepsy fumbled nervously with the several glasses of lemonade which stood temptingly ready on the counter and glanced fearfully but admiringly at the genius of this magnificent enterprise.

It was the biggest moment in her poor little life and Pee-wee was a conquering hero. She placed the fudge within his reach and waited in terrible suspense to see him operate upon this giggling band of lost pilgrims.

Nearer and nearer the car came and now it poked its big nickel plated nose around the bend and advanced slowly, easily, along the narrow, grass grown way. It looked singularly out of place in that wild valley.

A low, melodious horn politely reminded Simeon Drowser, who stood gaping in the middle of the road, to withdraw to a safer gaping point. He retreated to the platform in front of the post office and consulted with Beriah Bungel, the village constable, about this sumptuous apparition.

Only a couple of hundred feet remained now between the refreshment parlor and this party of mirthful victims. If Pepsy's red hair had been short enough it would have stood on end; as it was her fingers tingled with mingled appeal and confidence in the head of the firm.

Would it stop? Oh, would it stop? The suspense was terrible.

"F—r—resh doughnuts!" called Pee-wee in a sonorous voice. "Ice cold lemonade! It's ice cold! Get your fudge here!"

Pepsy looked admiringly upon her hero. She would not have dared to obtrude into the negotiations which seemed at hand. She gazed wistfully at a half dozen girls in fresh, colorful, summer array as only a little red-headed orphan girl in a gingham dress can do. She gazed at the big, palatial touring car with eyes spellbound. It was thus that the Indians first gazed upon the ships of Columbus.

"Hot frankfurters," shouted Pee-wee from behind his counter. "They're all hot! Here you are. Get your fresh sweet cider! Five a glass. Doughnuts six for a dime. All fresh."

CHAPTER XV

SIX MERRY MAIDENS

"What kind of nuts did you say?" called a girl merrily, as the car stopped.

"Doughnuts," said Pee-wee.

"We thought maybe everybody here were nuts," laughed the man who was driving.

"I'd like a nice saucerful of ground glass," laughed one of the girls. "Can you serve carbon remover with it?"

"Oh, isn't he just too cute." another girl said.

"Could we get a little of your delicious tire tape, we're so hungry? What are you all going to drink, girls? We'll have six glasses of carbon remover, if you please, and, let's see, we'll have six plates of ice cream hot out of the oven."

"Do you think you can jolly me?" said the head of the firm. "I'll give you some carpet tacks to eat if you'd like them."

"Oh, wouldn't those be too scrumptious," another girl said. "Do you serve peanut glue with them?"

"I'll give you some fried fish-hooks," Pee-wee shot back with blighting sarcasm.

"Yes, but what we'd like most of all is the ground glass," said another girl. "Is it chocolate or vanilla flavor?" At which they all giggled, while the man smiled broadly.

"What flavor glass are you going to have, Esther?" a girl asked.

"Oh, I think I'll take cathedral glass," caroled forth another; "I think it's more digestible than window glass, if it's properly cooked." At which there was another chorus of laughter.

The terrible conqueror, who intended to subdue this bevy of giggling maidens and cast a blight upon their levity, stood behind his counter like a soldier making a last stand in a third line trench, while Pepsy, captivated by the mirthful assailants, laughed uncontrollably.

The head of this firm saw that this was no time for dallying measures, his own partner was laughing, and even Wiggle was barking uproariously at Pee-wee as if he had shamelessly gone over to the enemy.

"Oh, If, It's just—too—excruciatingly funny or anything!" one of the girls laughed. "I never in my life heard of such—Oh, look at him! Look at him! Hold me or I'll collapse!"

Pee-wee had come around from behind the counter, tripped on his long white apron and gone sprawling on the ground, and the faithless Wiggle, taking advantage of this inglorious mishap, started pulling on the apron with all his might and main. Loyal Pepsy was only human, and tears of laughter streamed down her cheeks, and the neighboring woodland echoed to the sound of the unholy mirth in the auto.

A large frying fork which Pee-wee used as a sort of magnet to attract trade was still in his hand and by means of this he caught his white paper cap as it blew away, piercing it as if it were a fresh doughnut. It was indeed the only instance of triumph for him in the tragic affair. He arose, with Wiggle still tugging at his apron, his face decorated with colorful earth, his eyes glaring defiance.

The driver of the auto, who seemed to be a kindly man, put an end to this unequal and hopeless struggle of the scout by ordering a round of lemonade and purchasing fifty cents' worth of doughnuts. "When you have a few minutes to spare," he said in a companionable undertone, "stroll up the road and look about; the scenery is beautiful."

"What do you mean?" Pee-wee demanded.

"And be sure to take some salted spark plugs with you in case you get lost in the woods," one of the girls chirped teasingly as the auto started.

And the victim distinctly heard another say, as the big car rolled away: "It's a shame to tease him; he's just too cute for anything. I could just kiss him. But it was so excruciatingly funny."

CHAPTER XVI

A REVELATION

"What are you laughing at?" Pee-wee demanded to know, as soon as he had regained his poise and dignity. "You're as bad as they are."

"I couldn't help laughing," Pepsy said remorsefully, "'specially when you fell down. You said you were going to handle them."

"That could happen to the smartest man," Pee-wee said in scornful reproval; "that could happen to—to—to Julius Caesar."

"He's dead, you ask Miss Bellison," said Pepsy timidly.

"That shows how much you know," said Pee-wee scornfully as he brushed off his clothing.

"Can't something be a kind of a thing that could happen to somebody who's dead if he was very smart, only if he wasn't dead. We got a dollar and ten cents from them, didn't we?"

"Yes, but—did you—did you—handle them?" Pepsy asked fearfully.

"There are different ways of handling people," Pee-wee said; "you can't handle people that are crazy, can you? I can handle scoutmasters even."

Pepsy was willing to believe anything of her hero and she said, "They were a lot of freshies and I hate them anyway."

Pee-wee did not trouble himself about what the man had said. His chief interest was the dollar and ten cents of working capital which they now had and how to invest it. In his enthusiasm he had been rather premature in his advertisement of auto accessories, and he now purposed to make good at least one of these announcements by commissioning Simeon Drowser to buy some ten-cent rolls of tire tape for him at Baxter City, whither Simeon went daily.

He started along the road to the post office where he hoped to catch Simeon before that worthy left for Baxter City. But he did not reach the post office. The first interruption to his progress was one of his own two-card signs staring him in the face from a roadside tree:

CHEWING GUM

FOR PUNCTURES

He paused scowling before this novel announcement.

His gaze then wandered to a fence on which he read the astounding words:

PANCAKES FOR

HEADLIGHTS

Alas, the ground glass which should have appeared in place of pancakes did duty beneath the single word EAT on another tree nearby. Eat GROUND GLASS the hungry motorist was blithely advised.

Nor was this the worst. As Pee-wee penetrated deeper into the woods the more terrible was the masquerade of his own enticing signs. His stenciled cards, deserting their lawful mates, had struck up ghastly unions with other cards proclaiming frightful items of refreshment to the appalled wayfarer who was reminded of NON-SKID BANANAS and advised that OUR PEANUT TAFFY STICKS LIKE GLUE. The faithless TIRE TAPE which should have surmounted the STICK LIKE GLUE card was nestling under the fatal EAT, while FRANKFURTERS COLD AND COOLING and ICE CREAM SIZZLING HOT met Pee-wee's astonished gaze. He stood looking at this awful sequel of his handiwork.

Most of the cards were besmeared with mud and one or two in such a freakish way as to give a curious turn to their meaning. On one card a mischievous little rivulet of mud or wetted ink had ingeniously changed a T into a crude R and the travelers read RUBES SOLD HERE.

Pee-wee contemplated this exhibition with dismay. Wherever he looked, on fence or tree, some ridiculous sign stared him in the face. He did not continue on to the post office but retraced his steps to the refreshment parlor which was the subject of these printed slanders.

He and Pepsy were discussing this miscarriage of their exploitation design when a shuffling sound in the distance proclaimed the shambling approach of the advertising department. And if Pee-wee had not made good his flaunting boast to handle the six merry maidens, he at least made amends and regained somewhat of his heroic tradition in his handling of Licorice Stick.

"What did I tell you to do?" he shouted, his face red with terrible wrath. "What did I tell you to do? Do you know the way you put those cards up? You made fools of us, that's what you did!"

"I done gone make no fools of you, no how:" Licorice Stick exclaimed. "I see a sperrit 'n I shakes like dat, I do. As shu I'm stan' here I see a sperrit in dem woods."

From a vivid and terrifying narrative the partners made out that while Licorice Stick was on his way to embellish the wayside in strict accordance with instructions, he had encountered a spirit from the other world in the form of the carnival clown whom we have seen pass our wayside rest.

The ghostly raiment of this lowly humorist and the motley decoration of his face had so frightened Licorice Stick that he had dropped his cards and retreated

36

frantically into the woods. When the awful apparition had passed he hid stealthily shuffled back to the spot and with many furtive glances about him had gathered up the cards with trembling hands, and proceeded to post them in pairs without regard to their proper order.

After this triumphant exploitation feat (which ought to commend him to every lying advertiser in the world) Licorice Stick had shuffled into a new path of glory, going to the carnival, where (not finding the sperrit in evidence) he had accepted a position to stand behind a piece of canvas with his head in an opening and allow people to throw baseballs at him.

On hearing this Pee-wee desisted from any further criticism. For, as he told Pepsy, "a scout has to be kind and forgiving, and besides when I go to the carnival I can plug him in the face with a baseball two or three times and then we'll be square."

CHAPTER XVII

HARD TIMES

If many people went to the carnival they must have approached it from the other direction. It was a small carnival and probably did not attract much interest outside of Berryville. A few stragglers passed Mr. Quig's farm traveling in buckboards and farm wagons, but they did not come from distant parts and evidently were not hungry.

Some were so unscrupulous as to bring their lunches with them. One reckless farmer, indeed, bought a doughnut and exchanged it for another with a smaller hole.

Altogether the neighboring carnival did not bring much business to Pee-wee and Pepsy. Aunt Jamsiah took their enterprise good-naturedly; Uncle Ebenezer said it was a good thing to keep the children out of mischief. Miss Bellison, the young school teacher, bought ten cents' worth of taffy each day as a matter of duty, and Beriah Bungel, the town constable, being a natural born grafter, helped himself to everything he wanted free of charge.

So the pleasant summer days passed and brought them little business. Occasionally some lonely auto would crawl along the foliage-arched road, its driver looking for a place to turn around so that he might get back out of his mistaken way.

Most of these were too disgruntled at their mistakes and the quality of the road to heed the voice of the tempter who shouted at them, "Lemonade, ice cold! Get your lemonade here!" They usually answered by asking how they could get to West Baxter. And Pee-wee would answer, "You have to go four miles back, get your hot doughnuts here." Then they would start back but they never, never got their hot doughnuts there.

If Pee-wee's stout heart was losing hope he did not show it, but Pepsy
was frankly in despair. In her free hours she sat in their little
shelter, her thin, freckly hands busy with the worsted masterpiece that
she was working. Pee-wee, at least, had his appetite to console him, but
she had no relish for the stale lemonade and melting, oozy taffy which
stood pathetically on the counter each night.

One day a lumbering, enclosed auto went by, an undertaker's car it
was, and Pepsy was seized with sudden fright lest it be the orphan
asylum wagon come to get her. The two dominating thoughts of her simple
mind were the fear that she would have to go back to "that place" and
the hope that Pee-wee might get the money to buy those precious tents.
She had learned something of scouting, that scouts camp and live in
the open, and she had learned something of the good scout laws. She was
witnessing now an exhibition of scout faith and resolution, of faith
that was hopeless and resolution that was futile. She was soon to be
made aware of another scout quality which fairly staggered her and left
her wondering.

CHAPTER XVIII

THE VOICE OF THE TAIL-LIGHT

One night after dark, Pepsy and Pee-wee were sitting in their little roadside pavilion because they preferred it to the lamp-lighted kitchen smelling of kerosene where Uncle Ebenezer read the American Farm Journal, his arms spread on the red covered table.

A cheery little cricket chirped somewhere in this scene of impending failure; nearby a katydid was grinding out her old familiar song as if it were the latest popular air. In the barn across the yard the discordant sound of the horses kicking the echoing boards sounded clear in the still night and seemed a part of the homely music of the countryside.

Suddenly a speeding auto, containing perhaps its load of merry, heedless joy riders, went rattling over the old bridge along the highway and the loose planks called out across the interval of woodland to the little red-headed girl in this remote shack along the obscure by-road.

```
        "You have to go back,
         You have to go back,
         You have to go back."
```

Little did those speeding riders know of the voice they had called up to terrify this unknown child. The rattling, warning voice ceased as suddenly as it had begun as the unseen car rolled noiselessly along the smooth highway.

"Don't you be scared of it," Pee-wee said.

"You're as bad as Licorice Stick. Those old boards don't know what they're talking about. I wouldn't be scared of what anything said unless it was alive, that's sure."

"They voted not to build a new bridge for two years because they've got to build a new schoolhouse," said Pepsy. "That's because this county hasn't got much money. I'll be glad when they build it; the floor's going to be made out of stone; like—"

"You mean the bridge?"

"Yes, and I wish they'd hurry up. Every night I hear that and I know boards tell the truth, because if a door squeaks that means you're going to get married."

"All you need is an oil can to keep from getting married then," said Pee-wee, "because if you oil a door it won't squeak. So there; lets hear you answer that argument."

There was no answer to that argument; keeping single was just a matter of lubrication; but just the same that appalling sentence which had become fixed in Pepsy's mind, haunted her, especially when she lay on her feather mattress in the yellow painted bed up in her little room.

She was just about to go in when they were aroused by a sound in the distance. Pee-wee thought it was an auto and he made ready to deliver his usual verbal assault to the travelers.

Louder and louder grew the sound and suddenly a motorcycle with no headlight went whizzing past in the darkness. It was followed by another, also without any headlight, but this second rider stopped a little distance beyond the shack and got off his machine.

Something, he knew not what, dissuaded Pee-wee from making his customary announcements and he stood in the darkness watching this second speeder who seemed to be delayed by some trouble with his machine. The traveler was certainly too hurried and preoccupied to think of doughnuts.

Meanwhile, the first cyclist had covered perhaps fifty yards and was still going. The little red taillight of his machine shone brightly. Pee-wee was just wondering why these travelers used no headlights and whether the first cyclist would return to assist his friend, when he beheld something which caught and held his gaze in rapt concentration.

The little red taillight went out and on four times in quick succession. There followed an appreciable pause, then two quick flashes. Pee-wee watched the tiny light, spellbound. It appeared for a couple of seconds, then flashed twice with lightning rapidity.

"Hide," Pee-wee repeated to himself and motioned with his hand for Pepsy not to move. Now, in such rapid succession that Pee-wee could hardly follow them, the flashes appeared, tinier as the cyclist sped further away.

"Hide Kelly's barn," Pee-wee breathed.

Presently the second cyclist was on his machine again, speeding through the darkness. Either the first cyclist knew that his friend's trouble was not serious, or time was so precious that he could not pause in any case. Indeed, their flight must have been urgent to speed on such a road without headlights. The whole thing had a rather sinister look.

Pee-wee wondered who Kelly was and where his barn was located.

CHAPTER XIX

THE OTHER VOICE

"What do you mean, hide in Kelly's barn?" Pepsy whispered, greatly agitated.

"Can you keep still about it?" Pee-wee said.

"Girls can't keep secrets. Can you keep still till I tell you it's all right to speak?"

"I can keep a secret and not even tell it to you," she shot back at him in spirited defiance. "I know a secret that will—that will—help us sure to make lots and lots of money. And I wouldn't even tell you or Aunt Jamsiah, because she tried to make me. So there, Mr. Smarty. And I don't care whether you tell me or not if I can't keep a secret, but I've got a secret all by myself and it's that much bigger than yours," she said, spreading out her thin, little arms to include a vast area. "And besides that, I hate you," she added, bursting into tears and starting for the house. "And you can have that girl who was kept in after school for a partner," he heard her sobbing as she crossed the yard.

Pepsy did not pause to speak with Uncle Eb and Aunt Jamsiah who were sitting in the kitchen, but the latter, seeing her in tears, said kindly, "No folks passed by to the carnival to-night, Pepsy?"

"Looks like rain," Uncle Eb said consolingly; "to-morrer'll be the big night when they have the wrestlin' match. I reckon Jeb Collard n' all his summer folks will go up on th' hay-rig from West Baxter. You wait till to-morrer night, Pep. Mamsy'll make you up a pan of fresh doughnuts fer to-morrer night, won't you, Mamsy? Don't you take on now, Pepsy girl; you jes' go ter bed n' ferget yer troubles."

"I don't care about people from West Baxter," Pepsy said, stamping her foot and shaking her, head violently, "and I don't care about the old carnival or anything—so now. They're all too stingy—to—to—buy things—they're too stingy. I—I—I—don't care," she went on fairly in hysterics, "he says I can't—I can't—keep—keep—a secret—but I've got one and I won't tell it to anybody and I thought it up all myself and it will surely make lots and lots and lots of people come and buy—and—and he'll see if girls can do things." She was crying violently and shaking like a leaf.

"What is the secret, Pepsy?" Aunt Jamsiah asked gently; "maybe I can help you." "I won't tell—I won't tell anybody," Pepsy sobbed.

They were accustomed to these outbursts of her tense little nature and said no more. Pepsy went up to her little room under the eaves, catching each breath and trembling. No wonder they had not understood her at that big brick orphan home. No wonder she had hated it. Little as she was, she was too big for it.

She was in a mood to torment herself that night and she lay awake to listen for that dread voice from across the woods. She lay on her left side so they would have good luck next day. She was greatly overwrought and when at last she did hear the sound, loud and heartless with its sudden beginning and sudden end, it startled and terrorized her as if it were indeed that gloomy, windowless equipage of the State Orphan Home, coming to take her away.

She pushed her little fingers into her ears so that she could not hear it. . . .

CHAPTER XX

AN OFFICIAL REBUKE

As for Pee-wee, his trouble was quite of another character. The dubious outlook for their great enterprise did not submerge his buoyant spirit. He had been the genius of many colossal enterprises, most of them falling short of his glowing predictions, and his ingenious mind passed from one thing to another with no lingering regrets.

He usually invested so much enthusiasm in organization that he had none left for maintenance. He did not stick at anything long enough to be disappointed in it; there were too many other worlds to be conquered. His heart was no longer in the refreshment parlor and he was already finding solace in becoming his own solitary customer, by eating the taffy which he could not sell.

There had been so few things in Pepsy's poor little life that she had put her whole intense little heart and soul in this and was resolved that this hero from the great world of Bridgeboro should buy the tents which in plain fact he had already forgotten about.

So it happened that while Pepsy was lying on her left side (one of Licorice Stick's prescriptions) to insure good luck for the morrow, Pee-wee was dangling his legs from the counter eating a doughnut.

What concerned him now was this mystery of the speeding cyclists. That was the big thing in his young life. He believed them to be fugitives. Their reckless speed, and the fact that they used no headlights, gave color to this delightful supposition. Little had they thought that this diminutive scout, unseen in the darkness, had read that message in the Morse Code with perfect ease. Hide Kelly's Barn. What did that mean?

If Pee-wee had liked Beriah Bungel, the Everdoze constable, he would have gone to him with this information. But he disliked Beriah Bungel with true scout thoroughness; he knew him to be officious, and swelling with self-importance and he was not going to put business in such a creature's way.

But the next morning something happened which showed Scout Harris in a new light. Going to the post office early in the morning, he saw a sign posted on the bulletin board and he read it with lively interest.

```
                    $250.00 REWARD


        for information leading to the arrest and
conviction of the
        thieves who stole two motorcycles from the
yard of Chandler's
        Motorcycle Repair Shop in Baxter City.


        The machines are Indian models bearing license
plates 2570
        and 92632. Both machines are comparatively
new.


        Communicate with Austin Sawyer,
        County prosecutor, County of Borden, Baxter
City.
```

This notice had evidently been brought down by the mail driver early in the morning and several distinguished citizens of Everdoze were gathered about commenting on it. It seemed certain that none of the Everdoze dozers had heard the motorcycles and surely no one in the village would have been any the wiser for seeing those quick, tiny flashes, which told so much to the scout.

"I heerd somethin' but 'twan't no motorcycles," said Nathaniel Knapp; "'twas a auto or I'm crazy."

Then spoke Beriah Bungel, sticking his thumbs into his suspenders so that his rusty-colored coat flapped open showing his imposing badge, "They wouldn' never come this way, they wouldn', when they got th' highway ter go on. They hit inter th' highway from Barter, that's what they done. Them fellers hez confederates waitin' across th' state line with Noo York license plates. They made th' line last night; them fellers gits as fur as they kin on the first go off. Waal, ha ow's refreshments?" he added, turning upon Pee-wee.

"You ought to know," Pee-wee piped up; "you took enough of them." Which caused a laugh among the store loungers.

"When I wuz a youngster if I sassed my elders I got the hickory stick," Beriah said. "Yes, and when you grew up you got the peppermint sticks and doughnuts and things," Pee-wee shot back.

At this Darius Dragg and Nathaniel Knapp laughed uproariously. Constable Bungel saw but one way out of his rather embarrassing situation and that was the old approved device of a box on the ears. The official slap sounded loud in the little post office and left Pee-wee's cheek and ear tingling.

"I'll learn yer how to answer back yer superiors," said Constable Bungel. "We don't relish sass from city youngsters daown here, you mind that. Naow yer git along a outer here n' tell yer uncle ter learn yer some manners n' respect fer th' law."

Pee-wee faced him, his cheek flushed, his eyes blazing. "You're a—you're a—coward—and a thief—that's what you are," he shouted. "You—you—haven't got brains enough to find two—two—motorcycles—you haven't—all you can do is stand around and eat things that other people are trying to sell! You're a coward and a—a fo—ol—and you owe us as much as—a—a dollar. You'd better button your coat up or you'll—you'll be stealing your own watch—you—you coward!"

With this rebuke, which left Beriah gaping, Pee-wee started home, holding a hand to his cheek. He was trying hard not to cry, not from pain, but from the indignity he had suffered. He had never known such a thing in all his life before. He felt shamed, humiliated. His whole sturdy little form trembled at the thought of such degradation at the hands of a stranger. . . .

CHAPTER XXI

SCOUT HARRIS FIXES IT

Perhaps you will say that Pee-wee was not a good scout to speak with such impudent assurance to his elders. But you are to remember what I told you about Pee-wee, that everything about him was tremendous except his size. He was not always the ideal scout in little things. He was a true scout in the big things.

When he reached the shack he found Pepsy waiting for him and he poured forth his grievance into her sympathetic ears. "I'll fix him all right," he said; "he's a coward, that's what he is, and he, needn't think I'm afraid of him. I'll get even with him all right. Whenever I make up my mind to do a thing I do it, that's one thing sure."

"Only we didn't make a success of our refreshment parlor," Pepsy ventured to say, "but just the same we're going to because—"

"What do I care about it?" Pee-wee vociferated. "I know a way to get two hundred and fifty dollars and that's more money than we'd ever make in this old place. And I'll have you for my partner just the same. I'm going to get two hundred and fifty dollars all at once."

"Can I see it when you get it?" Pepsy asked.

"You can have half of it because we're partners," Pee-wee said, recovering something of his former spirits as this new prospect opened before him.

"Can't we have the refreshment parlor any more?" Pepsy asked wistfully. "Because, honest and true, we're going to make lots and lots of money in it; I know a way—"

"Listen, Pepsy," Pee-wee said. "Do you know what the Morse Code is? It's the language they use when they telegraph. Scouts have to know all about that. Do you remember when I said hide Kelly's barn last night? That's what that first feller said to the other one who was stuck. Didn't you notice how his little red light kept flashing away up the road? That's what it meant. They're hiding in Kelly's barn and nobody knows it.

"There's a sign in the post office and it says they'll give two hundred and fifty dollars to anybody who tells where they are. Do you think I'd tell Beriah Bungel?" he added contemptuously. "I'm going to tell a man named Sawyer, he's the county prosecutor, he lives in Baxter City. Only we have to go right away. I'm going back with the mail car to Baxter. Do you want to go? If you do you have to hurry up."

The last time that Pepsy had appeared before an official—of—the—law she had been sent to the big brick building and she was naturally wary of prosecutors, judges and such people. Suppose Mr. Sawyer should order herself and Pee-wee to the gallows for meddling in these dark, mysterious matters. Pee-wee read this in her face.

"Don't be scared," he said manfully; "I wouldn't let anybody hurt you. My father knows a man that's a judge and he tells jokes and has two helpings of dessert and everything just like other people. Prosecutors aren't so bad, gee whiz, they're better than poison-ivy; they're better than school principals anyway, that's sure. You see, I'll handle him all right."

Pepsy's thoughts wandered to the six merry maidens whom Pee-wee had "handled" with such astounding skill. "Can't we have our refreshment parlor any more?" she asked, with a note of homesickness for the little place they had decorated with such high hope. "If you'll wait, if you'll wait as much as—two weeks—lots and lots and lots and lots of people will come—"

But Pee-wee was not to be deterred by sentiment and false hope. "Don't you want us to have two hundred and fifty dollars?" he asked scornfully. "Don't you want us to buy those tents?" This was too much for Pepsy. She grasped Pee-wee's hand, following him reluctantly, as she gave a wistful look back at their little wayside shelter. The "stock" had not been set out for the day and the bare counter made the place look forlorn and deserted as they went away.

"It's a blamed sight easier than running a refreshment parlor," Pee-wee said; "it's just like picking the money up in the street. All we have to do is to go to Mr. Sawyer's office and tell him and—"

"You have to go in first," said Pepsy.

Pee-wee's enthusiasm was contagious and Pepsy was soon keyed up to the new enterprise, even to the point of facing Mr. Sawyer. She had cautiously resolved, however, to remain close to the door of his office, so that she might effect a precipitate retreat at the first mention of an orphan asylum.

Whatever Pee-wee did must be right and she saw now that two hundred and fifty dollars won in the twinkling of an eye was better than life spent in the retail trade. Yet she could not help thinking wistfully and fondly of their little enterprise and its cosy headquarters.

They sat on a rock by the roadside waiting for the mailman's auto to come along. Once in that Pepsy felt that her fate would be sealed. She had never been away from Everdoze since she had first been taken there. Baxter City was a vast place which she had seen in her dreams, a place where people were arrested and run over and where the constables were dressed up like soldiers. She clung tight to Pee-wee's hand.

"I hate him, too," she said, referring to Beriah Bungel, "and it will serve him right if Whitie dies and I just hope he does, because his father hit you."

"Who's Whitie?" Pee-wee asked.

"He's Mr. Bungel's little boy and he's all white because he's sick, and they can't take him to a great big place in the city so they can make him all well again and it just serves him right and I'm glad they haven't got any money. Everybody says he's going to die and Licorice Stick knows he's going to die in a rainstorm on a Friday, that's what he said."

This information about a little boy who was so pale that they called him Whitie, and who was going to die in a rainstorm on a Friday was all new to Pee-wee.

"Licorice Stick is crazy," he said. "What does he know about dying? He never died, did he?" This brilliant argument appeared to impress Pepsy.

"If they took him to a hospital in New York then he wouldn't have to die because they could fix him," Pepsy said. "I heard Aunt Jamsiah say so. There are doctors there that can' fix people all well again."

"I bet I'm as good a fixer as they are," Pee-wee said; "I fixed lots of people; I fixed a whole patrol once."

"So they wouldn't die?"

"They thought they were smart but I fixed them."

"Fixing smarties is different," said Pepsy. "If people have something the matter with their hips you can't fix them. Because, anyway, if they're going to die on a Friday even snail water won't fix them."

"Snail water, what's that?"

"It's medicine made from snails; Licorice Stick knows how to make it. You have to stir it with a willow stick and then you get well quick."

"How can you get well quick when snails are slow?" Pee-wee asked. "That shows that Licorice Stick is crazy. It would be better to make it with lightning-bugs."

"Lightning-bugs mean there are ghosts around," said Pepsy, "the lightning-bugs are their eyes. But anyway, just the same, nobody can fix Whitie Bungel, because the doctor from Baxter said so, and he knows because he's got an automobile."

"Automobiles don't prove you know a lot," said Pee-wee.

"Just the same Whitie is going to die," said Pepsy, "and then you'll see, because when my mother didn't have any money she died, so there." Pee-wee did not answer; he appeared to be thinking. And so the minutes passed as they sat there on the rock by the roadside, waiting for the mailman's auto to take them to Baxter City.

"Do you say I can't fix it?" he finally demanded. "Maybe you think scouts can't fix things. They know first aid, scouts do. I can fix that little feller; maybe you think I can't. You come with me, I'll show you. Scouts—scouts can do things—they're better than snails and lightning-bugs. I'll show you what they can do; you come with me."

"Ain't you going to wait for the mailman?"

"No, I'm not. You come with me."

This apparent desertion of another cherished enterprise all in the one day, took poor Pepsy quite by storm. She did not understand the workings of Pee-wee's active and fickle mind. But she followed his sturdy little form dutifully as he trudged up the road and into a certain lane. On he went, like a redoubtable conqueror with Pepsy after him. To her consternation he went straight up to the kitchen door, yes, of Constable Beriah Bungel's humble abode! Pepsy stood behind him in a kind of daze and heard his resounding knock as in a dream. Then suddenly to her dismay and terror she saw Beriah Bungel himself standing in the open doorway looking fiercely down at the little khaki-clad scout.

"Mr. Bungel," she heard as she stood gaping and listening and ready to run at the terrible official's first move, "Mr. Bungel, if you want to know where those two fellers are that stole the motorcycles, they're hiding in Kelly's barn and I guess they'll stay there till dark. So if you want to go and get them you'll get two hundred and fifty dollars as long as you don't say who told you where they are."

Without another word he turned and trudged away along the path, Pepsy following after him, to astonished to speak.

CHAPTER XXII

FATE IS JUST

On that very morning Constable Bungel performed the stupendous feat which sent his name ringing through Borden County and established him definitely as the Sherlock Holmes of Everdoze.

Followed by the local citizenry, who marveled at his deductive skill,

he advanced against Kelly's barn in the outskirts of Berryville. Here,

perceiving evidences of occupation, he demanded admittance and on

being ignored he forced an entrance and courageously arrested two young

fellows who were hiding there waiting for the night to come.

It is painful to relate that in process of being captured one of

these youthful fugitives delivered a devastating blow upon the long nose

of the constable thereby unconsciously doing a good turn like a true

scout and repaying him in kind for his treatment of Pee-wee Thus it will

be seen that fate is just for, as Pee-wee explained to Pepsy, "He got

everything I wanted him to get, a punch in the nose and two hundred and

fifty dollars. And that shows how I got paid back for doing a good

turn, because if I hadn't given up that two hundred and fifty dollars

he wouldn't have got punched, so you see it pays to be generous and kind

like it says in the handbook."

The official pride of Beriah Bungel as he led his captives back to Everdoze to await transportation to Baxter City was somewhat chilled by the inglorious appearance of his face. There can be no pomp and dignity in company with a wounded nose and Beriah Bungel's nose was the largest thing about him except his official prowess.

"Don't tell anybody I told him," Pee-wee whispered to Pepsy, "or you'll spoil it all and they won't give him the money."

"Suppose he tells himself," Pepsy said.

But Officer Bungel did not tell of the keen eyes and scout skill which had put him in the way of profit and glory. For he was like the whole race of Beriah Bungels the world over, officious, ignorant, contemptible, grafting, shaming human nature and making thieving fugitives look manly by comparison.

Everdoze was greatly aroused by this epoch making incident. Even a few stragglers from Berryville followed the crowd back as far as Uncle Ebenezer's farm and Pee-wee tried to tempt them into the ways of the spendthrift with taffy and other delights which cause the reckless to fall. But it was of no use.

"I bet if there was a murder we could sell a lot," he said. "Motorcycle thief crowds aren't very big. If the town hall burned down I bet we'd do a lot of business. I wish the school-house would burn down, hey? Murders and fires, those, are the best, especially murders, because lots of people come."

"I like fires better," Pepsy said. "Lots and lots and lots of people go to fires."

"Yes, and they get thirsty watching them, too," said Pee-wee. "That's the time to shout, ice cold lemonade."

There was one person in Everdoze, and only one, who neither followed nor witnessed this triumphal march, which had something of the nature of a pageant. This was a little lame boy, very pale, who sat in a wheel chair on the back porch of the lowly Bungel homestead.

The house was up a secluded lane and did not command a view of the weeds and rocks of the main thoroughfare. This frail little boy, whose blue veins you could follow like a trail, had never seen or heard of Pee-wee Harris, scout of the first class (if ever there was one) and mascot of the Raven Patrol. He had indeed heard his father speak of "cuffing a sassy little city urchin on the ear," but how should he know that this same sassy little urchin had thrown away two hundred and fifty dollars?

Thrown it away? Well, let us hope not. Let us hope that those wonder workers in the big city succeeded in "fixing" him, as indeed they must have done, if they were as good fixers as Scout Harris. Let us hope that Licorice Stick had gotten things wrong (as we have seen him do once before) and that little Whitie Bungel did not die in a rainstorm on a Friday.

CHAPTER XXIII

WHERE THERE'S A WILL THERE'S A WAY

To translate some little red flashes of light and read a secret in them was utterly beyond the comprehension of poor Pepsy. Here was a miracle indeed, compared with which the prophecies and spooky adventures of Licorice Stick were as nothing. And to win two hundred and fifty dollars by such a supernatural feat was staggering to her simple mind.

Licorice Stick's encounters with "sperrits" had never brought him a cent. But deliberately to sacrifice this fabulous sum in the interest of a poor little invalid that he had never seen, made Pee-wee not only a prophet but a saint to poor Pepsy. If scouts did things like this they were certainly extraordinary creatures. To give two hundred and fifty dollars to a person who has boxed your ears and then to go merrily upon your way in quest of new triumphs, that Pepsy could not understand.

The whole business had transpired so quickly that Pepsy had only seen the two hundred and fifty dollars flying in the air, as it were, and now they were poor again, even before they had realized their riches. And there was Pee-wee sitting on the counter of their unprofitable little roadside rest, with his knees drawn up, sucking a lemon stick (which apparently no one else wanted) and discoursing on the subject of good turns generally. There seemed to be nothing in his life now but the lemon stick.

"You think girls can't do good turns, don't you?" Pepsy queried wistfully.

Pee-wee removed the lemon stick from his mouth, critically inspecting the sharp point which he had sucked it to. By a sort of vacuum process he could sharpen a stick of candy till it rivaled a stenographer's pencil.

"Do you know what reciprocal means?" he asked with an air of concealing some staggering bit of wisdom.

"It's a kind of a church," Pepsy ventured.

"That's Episcopal," Pee-wee said with withering superiority! Placing the lemon stick carefully in his mouth again. This action was followed by a sudden depression of both cheeks, like rubber balls from which the air has escaped. He then removed the dagger-like lemon stick again to observe it.

"If you have an apple and I have an apple and you give me yours, that's a good turn, isn't it? And if I give you mine that's another good turn, isn't it? And we're both just as well off as we were before. That's recip—" He had to pause to lick some trickling lemon juice from his chubby chin, "rical."

Pepsy seemed greatly impressed, and Pee-wee continued his edifying lecture. "I should worry about two hundred and fifty dollars because you saw how people always get paid back only sometimes it isn't so soon like with the apples. Everything always comes out all right," continued the little optimist between tremendous sucks, "and if you're going to get a punch in the nose you get it, and you can see how Mr. Bungel got paid back auto—what'd you call it?"

"Automobile?" Pepsy ventured.

"Automatically," Pee-wee blurted out, catching a fugitive drop of lemon juice as it was about to leave his chin. "Good turns are the same as bad turns, only different. Do you see? I bet you can't say automatically while you're sucking a lemon stick."

"Is it a—a scout stunt?" Pepsy asked. Pee-wee performed this astounding feat for her edification, catching the liquid by-product with true scout agility. Whether from scout gallantry or scout appetite, he did not put Pepsy to the test.

"I'm glad of it, anyway," she said, "because now we can stay here and have our store and there isn't anybody like that pros—like that Mr. Sawyer to be afraid of."

"Do you think I'm afraid of prosecutors?" Pee-wee demanded to know. "I'm not afraid of them any more then I'm afraid of June-bugs; I bet you're afraid of June-bugs."

"I'm not," she vociferated, tossing her red braids and looking very brave.

"Then why should you be afraid of prosecutors?"

"I wouldn't be afraid of anything that doesn't sting."

Pepsy said nothing, only thought. And Pee-wee said nothing, only sucked the lemon stick, observing it from time to time, as its point became more deadly.

"Maybe I'm not as brave as you are and can't do things and I'm scared of Baxter City, but I bet you. I can think up as good turns as you can, so there! And if you promise to stay here I'll make it so lots of people will come and you can buy the tents and that will be a good turn won't it? You said if you make up your mind to do a thing you can do it."

"I wouldn't take back what I said," said Pee-wee, finishing the lemon stick by a terrible sudden assault with his teeth.

"Well, then, so there, Mr. Smarty," she said with an air of triumph, "I'm going to do a good turn, you see, because I made up my mind to it good and hard, and we'll make lots and lots of money. So do you promise to stay here and keep on being partners? Do you cross your heart you will?"

If Pee-wee had been as observant of Pepsy as he was used to being of signs along a trail he might have noticed that her eyes were all ablaze and that her little, thin, freckly wrist trembled. But how should he know that his own carelessly uttered words had burned themselves into her very soul?

"If you make up your mind to do a thing you can do it."

CHAPTER XXIV

PEPSY'S ENTERPRISE

Pepsy knew the scouts only through Pee-wee. She knew they could do things that girls could not do. She must have been deaf if she did not hear this. She knew they walked with dauntless courage in great cities, and that they were not afraid of prosecutors.

They were strange, wonderful things to her. They possessed all the manly arts and some of the womanly arts as well. They could track, swim, dive, read strange messages in flashes of light, sacrifice appalling riches and think nothing of it. They could cook, sew, imitate birds, and read things in the stars. Pee-wee had not left Pepsy in the dark about any of these matters.

Pepsy knew that she could not aspire to be a scout. The young propagandist had forgotten to tell her of the Girl Scouts who can do a few things, if you please. But one thing Pepsy could do; she could worship at the feet of his heroic legion.

If all there was to doing things was making up your mind to do them, then could she not do a good turn as well as a boy? Surely Scout Harris, the wonder worker, could not be mistaken about anything. He had shown Pepsy, conclusively, how good turns (to say nothing of bad ones) are always paid back by an inexorable law. Punches on the nose, or kindly acts of charity and sweet sacrifice, it was always the same. ...

Pepsy had no money invested in their unprofitable enterprise, for she had no money to invest. Neither had she any capital of scout experience to draw upon. But one little nest egg she had. She had once made a small deposit in this staunch institution of reciprocal kindness. All by herself, and long before she had known of Pee-wee and the scouts, she had done a good turn.

According to the inevitable rule, which she did not doubt, the principal and interest of this could now be drawn. Why not? Somewhere, and she knew where, there was a good turn standing to her credit. It would be paid her just as surely as that splendid punch in the nose was paid to Beriah Bungel. And, using this good turn that was standing to her credit, she would be the instrument which fate would choose, to pay scout Harris back for his great sacrifice of two hundred and fifty dollars. You see how nicely everything was going to work out.

The person who would now do Pepsy the good turn which would bring success and fortune to their little enterprise and enable Scout Harris to buy three tents, was Mr. Ira Jensen who lived in the big red house up the road. A very mighty man was Mr. Ira Jensen almost as terrible in worldly grandeur and official power as a prosecutor. Not quite, but almost. At all events, Pepsy could muster up courage to go and face him, and that she was now resolved to do.

Indeed, this had been her secret.

CHAPTER XXV

AN ACCIDENT

Mr. Ira Jensen sometimes wore a white collar and he was deacon in the church and he was the one who selected the Everdoze school teacher, and he was president of the Horden County Agricultural Association and he had a khaki-colored swinging-seat on his porch and muslin curtains in his windows. So you may judge from all this what a mighty man he was.

Such a man is not to be approached except upon a well-considered plan. It required almost another week of idling in the refreshment parlor, of vain hopes, and ebbing interest on the part of the scout partner, to bring Pepsy to the state of desperation needed for her terrible enterprise. A sudden and alarming turn of Pee-wee's fickle mind precipitated her action.

"Let's eat up all the stuff and make the summerhouse into a gymnasium, and we can give magic lantern shows in it, too. What do you say?" Pee-wee inquired in his most enthusiastic manner. "We can charge five cents to get in." He did not explain whence the audiences would come. He had found an old magic lantern in the attic and that was enough. The only stock now on hand was what might be called the permanent stock (if any stock could be called permanent where Pee-wee was). No longer did the fresh, greasy doughnut and the cooling lemonade grace the forlorn little counter.

"No, I won't!" Pepsy said, tossing those red braids. "I won't eat the things because we started here and I love them, so there!"

"If you love them I should think you'd want to eat them," said Pee-wee. "That shows how much you know about logic."

"I don't care, I'm just going to stay here and if you promise to wait we'll get lots and lots of money," she said. "You promised me you'd wait," she added wistfully, "you crossed your heart. Won't you please wait till—till—five days—may-be? Won't you, please? Maybe that will be a good turn, maybe?"

He did not refuse. Instead he helped himself to some gumdrops out of a glass jar, and appeared to be content. But Pepsy knew better than to trust the fickle heart of man and that night she played the poor little card that she had been holding.

After Uncle Eb and Aunt Jamsiah had gone to bed and while the curly head of Scout Harris was reposing in sweet oblivion upon his pillow, Pepsy crept cautiously down the squeaky, boxed-in stairs and paused, in suspense, in the kitchen. The ticking of the big clock there seemed very loud, almost accusing, and Pepsy's heart seemed to keep time with it as it thumped in her little breast. How different the familiar kitchen seemed, deserted and in darkness! The two stove lids were laid a little off their places to check the banked fire, leaving two bright crescent lines like a pair of eyes staring up at her. This light, reflected in one of the milk pails standing inverted on a high shelf, made a sort of ghostly mirror in which Pepsy saw herself better than in that crinkly, outlandish mirror in her little room.

For a moment she was afraid to move lest she make a noise, and so she paused, almost terrified, looking at her own homely little face, on the most fateful night of her life. Then she tiptoed out through the pantry where the familiar smell of fresh butter reassured her. It seemed companionable, in the strange darkness and awful stillness, this smell of fresh butter. She crept across the side porch where the churn stood like a ghost, a dish-towel on its tall handle and crossed the weedy lawn, where the beehives seemed to be watching her, and headed for the dark, open road. But here her courage failed. Some thought of doing her errand in the morning occurred to her, but, she could not go then without saying where and why she was going. And in case of failure no one must ever know about this. ...

So she screwed up her courage and returned to the side porch to get a lantern. She shook it and found it empty. There was nothing to do now but brave the darkness or go down into the cellar and fill the lantern from the big kerosene can. She paused in the darkness before those sepulchral stone steps, then in a sudden impulse of determination she tightened her little hand upon the lantern till her nails dug into her palms and went down, down.

She groped her way to the kerosene can and finally came upon it and felt its surface. Yes, it was the kerosene can. Her trembling little hand fumbled for the tiny faucet. How queer it felt in the dark when she could not see it! It seemed to have a little knob or something on it. ...

Her hand was shaking but she held the little tank of the lantern under the faucet and was about to turn the handle when something—something soft and wet and silent—touched her other hand. She drew a quick breath, her heart was in her mouth, her hands were icy cold. Still she had presence of mind enough not to scream.

But as she rose in panic terror from her stooping posture, the lantern pulled upward against the faucet, toppling the big can off its skids. There was no plug in the can and the kerosene flowed out upon the terror-stricken child, wetting her shoes and stockings, and made a great puddle on the stone floor. She stood in the darkness, seeing none of this, which made the catastrophe the more terrible.

And then, as she stood in terror, wet and bewildered, waiting for whatever terrible sequel might come, she felt again that something soft and wet and silent on her hand. She moved her hand a little and felt of something soft. Soft in a different way. Soft but not wet.

"Wiggle," she sobbed in a whisper; "why—why—didn't you—you—tell me it was you—Wiggle?"

But he only licked her hand again as if to say, "If there is anything on for to-night, I'm with you. Cheer up. Adventures are my middle name". ...

CHAPTER XXVI

PEPSY'S INVESTMENT

For a few seconds Pepsy stood in suspense amid the spreading, dripping havoc she had caused, listening for some sound above. But the seconds piled up into a full minute and no approaching step was heard. The danger seemed over.

But the very air was redolent of kerosene; she stood in a puddle of it, and one of her stockings and both of her plain little buttoned shoes were thoroughly wet. When she moved her toes she could feel the soppy liquid. Oh, for a light! It would lessen her terror if she could just see what had happened and how she looked.

She groped her way to the small oblong of lesser darkness which indicated the open bulk-head doors, and felt better when she was in the free open darkness of outdoors. Wiggle, seeming to know that something unusual was happening, kept close to her heels.

She reentered the kitchen, where those accusing, ghostly, red slits of eyes in the stove seemed to watch her. She fumbled nervously on the shelf above the stove and got some matches, spilling a number of them on the floor. She could not pause to gather them up while those red eyes stared. She had planned her poor little enterprise with a view to secrecy, but in the emergency and with the minutes passing, she did not now pause to think or consider. Near the flour barrel hung several goodly pudding bags, luscious reminders of Thanksgiving. Aunt Jamsiah had promised to make a plum-pudding for Pee-wee in the largest one of these and he had spent some time in measuring them and computing their capacity, with the purpose of selecting the most capacious. Pepsy now hurriedly took all of these and a kitchen apron along with them, and descended again into the cellar.

By the dim lantern light she lifted the fallen tank and replaced it on its skids. Then she wiped up the floor as best she could with the makeshift mop which had been intended to serve a better purpose. She wiped off her soggy shoes and tried to clean that clinging oiliness from her hands. It seemed to her as if the whole world were nothing but kerosene.

She did not know what to do with the drenched rags, so she took them with her when she started again for the dark road, this time with her two cheery companions, the lantern and Wiggle. She soon found the dripping rags a burden and cast them from her as she passed the well. Wiggle turned back and inspected the smelly, soggy mass, found that he did not like it, took a hasty drink from the puddle under the well spout, and rejoined his companion.

It must have been close to ten o'clock when Mr. Ira Jensen, enjoying a last smoke on his porch before retiring, saw the lantern light swinging up his roadway. The next thing that he was aware of was the pungent odor of kerosene borne upon the freshening night breeze. And then the little delegation stood revealed before him, Wiggle, wagging his tail, the lantern sputtering, and

Pepsy's head jerking nervously as if she were trying to shake out what she had to say.

It took Pepsy a few moments to key herself up to the speaking point. Then she spoke tremulously but with a kind of jerky readiness suggesting many lonely rehearsals.

"Mr. Jensen," she said, "I have to do a good turn and so I came to ask

you if you'll help me and the reason I smell like kerosene is because

I tipped over the kerosene can." This last was not in her studied part,

but she threw it in answer to an audible sniff from Mr. Jensen.

"You said when I came here and stayed nights when Mrs. Jensen

was sick with the flu and everybody else was sick and you couldn't get

anybody to do—to nurse her—you remember?" She did not give him time to

answer for she knew that if she paused she could not go on. Her momentum

kept her going. "You said then—just before I went home—you'd—you said

I was—you said you'd do me a good turn some day, because I helped you.

So now a boy that's staying with us—we have a refreshment parlor and

nobody comes to buy anything—and he wants to buy some tents and we have

to make a lot of money so will you please have them have the County Fair

in Berryville this year so lots of people will go past our summerhouse?

"We have lemonade and he calls to the people and tells them, only there ain't any people. But lots and lots and lots of people come to the County Fair from all over, don't they? So now I'd like it for you to do me that good turn if you want to pay me back."

Thus Pepsy, standing tremulously but still boldly, her thin little hand clutching the lantern, played her one card for the sake of Pee-wee Harris, Scout. Standing there in her oil soaked gingham dress, she made demand upon this staunch bank of known probity, for principal and interest in the matter of the one great good turn she had one before she had ever known of Scout Harris. It never occurred to her as she looked with frank expectancy at Mr. Jensen that her naive request was quite preposterous.

To his credit be it said, Mr. Jensen did not deny her too abruptly. Instead he spread his knees and arms and, smiling genially, beckoned her to him.

"I can't, I'm all kerosene," she said.

"Never you mind," he said. "You come and stand right here while I tell you how it is." So she set down the lantern and stepped forward and stood between his knees and then he lifted her into his lap. "Well, well, well, you're quite a girl; you're quite a little girl, ain't you, huh? So you came all the way in the dark to ask me that! Here, you sit right where you are and never you mind about kerosene; if you ain't scared of the dark I reckon I ain't scared of kerosene. Now, I want you should listen 'cause I'm going to tell you jes' how it is n' then you'll understand. Because I call you a little kind of a—a herro—ine, that's what I call you."

He wasn't half wrong about that, either. ...

CHAPTER XXVII

SEEN IN THE DARK

So then he told her how it was about the County Fair, which shortly would open. He told her very gently and kindly how Northvale had been chosen, because it was the county seat and how he was powerless to change the plans.

He looked around into her sober face, and sometimes lifted it to his, and at almost every hope-blighting sentence, asked her if she did not understand. He told her all about how county fairs are big things, planned by many men, months and months in advance. And at each pause and each gently asked question she nodded silently, as if it was all quite clear and plausible, but her heart was breaking.

"But I'm not going to forget that good turn I owe you, no, siree," he added finally as he set her down on the porch, much to Wiggle's relief. "And I'm coming down the road to pay you a visit n' look over that refreshment store of yours n' see if I can't make some suggestions maybe. Now, what do you say to that?"

Pepsy nodded soberly, her thoughts far away.

"You'll see me along there," Mr. Jensen added cheerily, as he patted her little shoulder, "n' I give you fair warning I'm the champion doughnut eater of Borden County."

She smiled, still wistfully, and gulped, oh ever so little.

"That's what I am," he added with another genial pat. "So now you cheer up and run back home and go to bed n' don't you lie awake crying. You tell that little scout feller I'm coming to make you a visit n' that, I usually drink nine glasses of lemonade. Now you run along and get to bed quick."

"Thanks," she said, her voice trembling.

So Pepsy took her way silently along the dark road. Her bank had failed, she could do nothing more. This was a strange sequel to follow Pee-wee's glowing representations about good turns. She did not understand it. And now that she had failed, the catastrophe in the cellar loomed larger, and she saw her nocturnal truancy as a serious thing. What would Aunt Jamsiah think of this? Pepsy had been forbidden to go away from the farm at night, except to weekly prayer meeting.

The crickets sang cheerily as she returned along the dark road, a disconsolate little figure, swinging her lantern. She was weary—weary from exertion and disappointment and foreboding. Her good scout enterprise was suddenly changed into an act of sneaking disobedience. The physical exhaustion which follows nervous strain was upon her now and her little feet lagged in their soaking shoes and once or twice she stumbled with fatigue.

For what burden is heavier than a heavy heart? The soothing voices of insect life which soften the darkness and cheer the wayfarer in the countryside seemed only to mock her with their myriad care-free songs. And to make matters worse there suddenly rang in her ears from far over to the west the loud clatter of those loose planks on the old bridge along the highway, as a car sped over it:

"You have to go back,

You have to go back."

Then the noise ceased suddenly, and there was no sound but the calling of a screech-owl somewhere in the intervening woods.

Pepsy sat down on a rock by the roadside partly to rest and partly because she did not want to go home. She knew, or she ought to have known, that Aunt Jamsiah was pretty sure to be lenient about a harmless transgression with so generous a motive. But the warning voice from that unseen bridge disconcerted her. It was not long after she was seated that her head hung down and soon the gentle comforter of sleep came to her and she lay there, pillowing her head on her little thin arm.

But the comforter did not stay long, for Pepsy dreamed a dream. She dreamed that all the people of the village, Simeon Drowser, Nathaniel Knapp, Darius Dragg, the sneering Deadwood Gamely, and even the faithless Arabella Bellison, the school teacher, were pointing fingers a yard long, at her and saying, "You have to go back to the big brick building. You have to go back, you have to go back." On the big doughnut jar in the "refreshment parlor" sat Licorice Stick saying, "You have to go back the next time it thunders." She shook her fist at Licorice Stick and called him a Smarty and said she would not go back, but they all laughed and sang:

"You have to go back,

You have to go back."

Miss Bellison was the worst of all. ...

57

<pre>
"You have to go back,
  You have to——"
</pre>

With a sudden start Pepsy sat up on the rock, wide awake,

<pre>
"——-go back,
  You have to go back.",
</pre>

She still heard.

Her forehead throbbed and her face felt very hot. There was a ringing in her ears. She was feverish, but she did not know that. All she knew was that everybody was against her and that the bridge had put them up to it. She was dizzy and had to put her hand on the rock to steady herself. The lantern light was extinguished but she did not remember the lantern, or Wiggle. She felt very strange and wanted a drink of water. Her hand trembled and her little arm with which she braced herself against the rock, felt weak. And her head throbbed, throbbed. ...

Where were all those people? She felt around for them. Then she heard the voice again, far off through the woods, up along that highway. It was just an innocent automobile,

<pre>
"You have to go back."
</pre>

Pepsy rose to her feet with a start, reeled, reached for a tree, and clutched it. "I'll stop it, I'll—I'll make it—it stop—I'll tear it—I'll pull them off," she said. "I—I won't—go back—I won't, I won't, I won't!"

Staggering across the road she entered the woods. Each tree there seemed like two trees. She groped her way among them, dizzy, almost falling. Sometimes the woods seemed to be moving. Perhaps it was by the merest chance that she stumbled into the trail which led through the woods to the highway, ending close to the old bridge.

But once in the familiar path she ran in a kind of frenzy. No doubt the fever gave her a kind of temporary, artificial strength, as indeed it gave her the crazy resolve somehow to still that haunting voice forever. Crazed and reeling she stumbled and ran along, pausing now and again to press her throbbing head, then running on again like one possessed.

At last she came out of the woods suddenly on to the broad, smooth highway. There was the bridge, silent and—no, not dark. For there was a bright spot somewhere underneath it and gray smoke wriggling up through those cracks between the planks. And there, yes, there, crawling away in the darkness was a black figure. A silent, stealthy figure, stealing away.

To the dazed, feverish girl, the figure seemed to have two pairs of arms. She tried to call but could not. Her scream of delirious fright died away into a murmur as she staggered and fell prone upon the ground and knew no more.

But never again—never, never would those cruel planks taunt her with their heartless prediction. Never would they frighten the poor, sensitive, fearful little red-headed orphan girl any more.

CHAPTER XXVIII

STOCK ON HAND

It was Joey Burnside, the burliest and heartiest of the volunteer firemen, who carried Pepsy back through the woods to the farm while still the conflagration was at its height.

There was not timber enough left from the old bridge to kindle a scout camp-fire. A few charred remnants had gone floating down the stream and these fugitive remnants drifting into tiny coves and lodging in the river's bends were shown by the riverside dwellers as memorials of the event which had stirred the countryside more than any other item, of neighborhood history. Under the gaping space of disconnected road the stream flowed placidly, uninterrupted by all the recent hubbub above it. The straight highway looked strange without the bridge.

Pepsy had a fever all that night, but toward morning she fell asleep, and Aunt Jamsiah, who had watched her through the night, tiptoed into the little room under the eaves and out again to tell Pee-wee that he had better wait, that all Pepsy needed now was rest.

"Can't I just look at her?" Pee-wee asked. So he was allowed to stand in the doorway and see his partner as she lay there sleeping the good sleep of utter exhaustion.

"When she wakes up," Aunt Jamsiah said pleasantly.

Pee-wee knew the circumstances of her being found at the burning bridge and brought home, but he asked no questions and Aunt Jamsiah said nothing of the events of that momentous night. It seemed to be generally understood that this matter was in Aunt Jamsiah's hands for thorough consideration later.

Meanwhile Pee-wee went across the lawn and down the road to the scene of their hapless enterprise. The roadside rest could boast now of but two jars, one of peppermint sticks and one of gumdrops (both in rapid process of consumption) and a number of spools of tire tape. But the absence of doughnuts and sausages and lemonade, this was nothing. It was the absence of Pepsy that counted.

Pee-wee took his customary eye-opener, consisting of a gumdrop. He had to shake the jar to get a red one, that being the kind he preferred. Then he drew his legs up on the counter and proceeded to work upon the willow whistle he was making.

His handiwork soon reached that stage of manufacture where it was necessary to soak the willow bark in water, so as to cause it to swell. He thereupon distributed the remaining gumdrops impartially between his mouth and his trousers pocket and filled the empty jar with water, dropping his handiwork into it. Thus by gradual stages and without any sensational "closing out sales" the refreshment business was steadily going into a state of liquidation, even the lemon sticks being reduced to a liquid. There was no stock on hand now but two peppermint sticks and some tire tape.

Suddenly a most astonishing thing happened. The sound of an automobile horn was heard in the distance. A deep, melodious, dignified horn. Not since the passing of the six merry maidens had such welcome music sounded in Pee-wee's enraptured ears.

The signs had all been made fight, the ice cream had been made cold, the sausages hot, and the ground glass had been put where it belonged. No longer did "our taffy stick like glue." Indeed, there was no taffy of any kind on hand, notwithstanding these blatant announcements.

Along came the automobile, an eight-cylinder Super Junkster. And, yes, it was followed by another, and still another. Pee-wee could see the imposing procession as far down as the bend.

"Some detour," a good-natured voice said.

"Detour? Detour?" Pee-wee whispered in sudden and terrible excitement. Then, as the full purport of the staggering truth burst upon him he issued forth from the roadside rest and contemplated the approaching pageant with joy bubbling up like soda water in his heart.

"Never mind," said another voice, "we can get some eats in this jungle, thank goodness. What I won't do to a couple of hot frankfurters."

A sudden chill cooled the fresh enthusiasm of Scout Harris.

"I'll buy every blamed doughnut they've got in the place," somebody shouted. "We won't leave a thing for the rest of the cars that have to plow through this jungle. I suppose this is what motorists will be up against for six months. What do you know about that? This eats merchant ought to clear a couple of million. I'll dicker with him for everything hot that he's got, I'm starving."

"Same here!" another shouted.

Frantically, like a soldier waving his country's emblem in the last desperate moment of forlorn hope Scout Harris clambered over the counter and grasped the jar containing two peppermint sticks.

"Peppermint sticks! Peppermint sticks!" he shouted at the advancing column. "Get your peppermint sticks! They quench thirst and—and—and satisfy your hunger! They're filling! They warm you up! Peppermint is hot! Oh, get your peppermint sticks here!"

CHAPTER XXIX

INDUSTRIAL CONDITIONS

Pee-wee emerged safely, if not triumphantly, from this ordeal amid much laughter, and was just congratulating himself upon his skillful handling of "the trade" in a period of acute shortage when he received a knockout blow. In depositing the trifling price of the peppermint sticks in his trousers pocket, he discovered there four gumdrops glued together and clinging so affectionately that nothing could part them.

At the moment of this discovery, Scout Harris, thus driven into a corner and standing at bay with nothing but one huge, consolidated gumdrop for defense, heard the unmistakable sound of another car crawling over the rocks and hubbles of that outlandish road in second gear. On, on, on, it came like some horrible British tank.

And now again he heard voices, "We can eat about twenty of them in my patrol y—mm. Are we hungry? Oh, no! Hot frankfurters! Oh, boy, lead me to them. I could even eat the sign, I'm so hungry. Put her in high. What do we care about the road?"

Pee-wee listened and waited in terrible suspense. Scouts! He knew something about the scout capacity. Then, upon the fresh morning air there floated another voice calling a sentence which he knew too well it was the good scout motto. "Hey there, you, whoever you are, Mr. Refreshment Man? Be Prepared! We're s—c—o—u—t—s we are and we're h—u—n—g—r—e—e! We haven't had anything since breakfast at four-thirty. We had to come around through this rocky tour or detour or whatever you call it. Somebody ate the bridge last night. Are there any scouts down in this South African backyard?"

If Pee-wee had not heard that familiar motto "Be Prepared," he would have known the approaching caravan to be scouts by their talk and banter.

Be Prepared. Pee-wee glanced at the bare counter and the empty jars and the shiny dishpan which held nothing but Pepsy's ball of worsted and the terrible ornamental thing that she was knitting. There they were, just as she had laid them the day before. Poor little Pepsy. ...

Then they descended upon him as only hungry scouts can descend. Pee-wee's glowing promises which decorated the woods (and which he could not fulfill) had brought the party to a state of distraction. It was a big Crackerjack touring car overflowing with scouts and driven by a smiling scoutmaster. It seemed as if they ought to have been pressed in and down with a shovel like ice cream in a quart box.

"For the love of—" one of them began.

"Look what's here, it's a scout."

"That?" shouted another, "Let's have the magnifying glass, will you?"

Pee-wee straightened himself up to his full height. The big Crackerjack touring car stopped.

"Some detour," the scoutmaster said with an air of infinite relief.

"Do they have scouts down here?" a member of the party asked.

"I'm only staying here, I belong in Bridgeboro, New Jersey," Pee-wee said.

"Don't talk about bridges," another scout said.

"Talk about something pleasant. A scout is supposed to save life, scout law number six; let's have a couple of thousand hot dogs, will you? We're dying. And forty-eleven dozen doughnuts with the holes removed."

"Do you—I—eh—do you—need any tire tape?" Pee-wee stammered, playing for time. "Tire tape! What do you take us for? A lot of blow-outs? Let's have some eats and we'll take care of the blow-out."

"Come on, hurry up, a scout is supposed to be prepared," piped up a natty scout wearing the bronze cross.

"Where's all the food?" the scoutmaster asked, glancing at the empty counter. "We were led to suppose—"

"Don't you know what a shortage is?" Pee-wee piped up in sheer desperation.

"We know what a shorty is," one of the party shot back.

"You don't expect us to eat a shortage, do you?" another said. "Come ahead, hurry up, a scout isn't supposed to be cruel. You can always depend on scout signs that you find in the woods. A scout that puts scout signs—"

"Those are different kinds of signs!" Pee-wee shouted. "Those are trail signs. You think you're so smart! That shows how much you know about—about—"

"Three strikes out," one of the scouts shouted. "About—about industrial conditions," Pee-wee concluded. "Don't you know what a—a—what'd you call it—a—"

"Yes, that's what you call it," a scout laughed.

"Don't you know what a reconstruction period is?" Pee-wee fairly yelled, amid uncontrollable laughter. "If something happens like a war—or a—a bridge burning down—or something—or other—that makes business conditions— what'd you call it—it makes them all kind of upside down, doesn't it? Sometimes—kind of—things are hard to get. Everybody knows that."

"We can see it," a scout said.

By this time the scoutmaster was laughing heartily but with the greatest good humor. Pee-wee continued bravely, to the great amusement of the party.

"Gee whiz, nobody ever came along this road. You admit that scouts are hungry, don't you?"

"We proclaim it," said the scoutmaster.

"I ate a lot of the stuff and my aunt wouldn't cook any more stuff for us because nobody ever came and it got stale and I ate too much of it, that's what she said. So now, anyway, we're going to start in again because the business world—and we're—we're going to speed up production."

"All right, speed up the auto and good luck to you," the scout with the bronze cross said. He seemed to be a patrol leader.

There was a little fraternal chat before this boisterous troop moved on and all seemed interested in Pee-wee and his enterprise. They were on their way to camp somewhere down the line. "You'll succeed all right," they called back to him, "only be sure to have plenty of stuff on hand when we come back in a couple of weeks or we'll kill you."

"Do you like waffles and honey?" the proprietor shouted after them.

"We've got the bees working overtime for us," a scout called back.

"I'll have a lot of those—ten cents each," Pee-wee announced. "Do you like clam chowder?" he called, raising his voice to cover the increasing distance.

"Don't you make us hungry," one called back.

"Good luck to you, you'll make it a go all right."

"I'm lucky, I always have good luck," the small optimist screamed at the top of his voice. "Do you like peanut taffy? Do you like hot corn," he added, fairly yelling this sudden inspiration after the departing sufferers; "with butter and pepper on it; do you like that? I'll have some!"

These were the last words they heard as the big car moved slowly over the rocky, grass-grown road. They are good words to end a chapter with—hot corn with pepper and butter on it. ...

Oh, boy!

CHAPTER XXX

PAID IN FULL

Pee-wee was just about to make a frantic rush to the house when he saw another automobile coming along the road, brushing the projecting foliage aside as some stealthily advancing creature might do. Not far behind it he could hear other ears grinding along that impossible road in second gear.

The world seemed to be making a pathway, of rather a highway, to Pee-wee's door. The sequestered, overgrown road, with its intertwined and overarching boughs, was become a surging thoroughfare. The birds, formally unmolested in their wonted haunts, complained to one another of this sudden intrusion into their domains. Away back where this obscure road branched off the highway to furnish the unfrequented access to Everdoze and Berryville, a sign had been placed that morning with an arrow pointing toward the depths of the Everdoze jungle.

DETOUR —>

HIGHWAY CLOSED. FOLLOW
YELLOW ARROWS.

These yellow arrows appeared at intervals along the Everdoze road, thus guiding the motorist back to the highway at a point a mile or two below the gap where the bridge had been. Everdoze was on the map now in dead earnest. The little hamlet nestling in its wooded valley was destined to review such a procession of Pierce-Arrows, and Packards, and Cadillacs, aye and Fords and jitney busses, as it had never dreamed of in all its humble career.

Who was responsible for this? Or was accident responsible? Who, if anyone, by the mere touching of a match had started a blaze which, would illuminate poor little Everdoze? Everdoze had gone to bed (at eight P. M.) in obscurity. It had awakened to find itself dragged into the light of day. Already Constable Bungel was devising a formidable code of "traffic regulations"—traps and snares to catch the prosperous and make them pay tribute as they passed along.

As early as seven o'clock that vigilant agent of the peace had placed a sign in front of the post office (where he was wont to loiter) reading, "NO PARKING HERE." But all the while he hoped that the unwary would park there and pay the three dollars and costs.

But of all the signs which appeared in Everdoze on that day when fate, like an alarm clock, had awakened it out of its slumber, there was one which thrilled the soul of Pee-wee Harris and caused consternation to everybody else. This appeared in front of the "Town Hall" and at a number of other strategic places in and out of the village.

"Come and read it! Come and read it!" shouted little Silas Knapp as he madly intercepted Pee-wee who, as I have said, was about to run to the house. "It's a monolopy or somethin' like that—Mr. Drowser says so! Come and read it!"

So before going to the house Pee-wee went and read it. He did not know that the stern phraseology had been penned ever so tenderly and with a twinkle in the eye, of the writer. He did not know that it was a tribute (or shall we say the repayment of a good turn?) to the little red-headed girl, who, all unaware of this hubbub, was sleeping in her little bedroom under the eaves. Strange that such a little girl could thus shake her fist by proxy at the grasping villagers!

NOTICE

```
                    The property on both sides of the
road
                    from two miles north of the Everdoze
line to       .
                    the boundary of Ebenezer Quig's farm,
is of
                    private ownership.

                    Anyone attempting to sell or vend or
who
                    erects any tent or shack for such
purpose upon
```

said property will be prosecuted to the full

extent of the law.

IRA C. JENSEN.

So Pepsy had kept her word after all, her one poor little investment of kindness had paid a hundred percent dividend, and the partners were the owners of a monopoly, or a monolopy, whichever you choose to call it.

CHAPTER XXXI

CIRCUMSTANTIAL EVIDENCE

Along the road and over the stone wall and straight across the bed of tiger-lilies sped Pee-wee, using his own particular mode of scout pace, patent not applied for. Across the side porch and into the kitchen he went, pell-mell, shouting in a voice to crack the heavens.

"It's a monolopy—I mean a monopoly! We've got a monopoly! Where's everybody? Hey, Aunt Jamsiah, where are you? Where's Uncle Eb? Hurry up and make some doughnuts? There's a detour! Cars—hundreds of cars—from the highway—they're coming along the road. You ought to see. Where's the ice-pick? Can I have some lemons? Are there any cookies left? I left two on the plate last night. Where's the sugar so I can—"

He paused in his frenzy of haste and enthusiasm as Aunt Jamsiah opened the sitting room door, very quietly and seriously.

"Shh, come in here, Walter," she said.

Her manner, kind, gentle, but serious, disconcerted Pee-wee and chilled his enthusiasm. The very fact that he was summoned into the sitting room seemed ominous for that holy of holies was never used; not more than once or twice in Pee-wee's recollection had his own dusty shoes stood upon that sacred oval-shaped rag carpet. Never before had he found himself within reaching distance of that plush album that stood on its wire holder on the marble table.

This solemn apartment was the only room in the house that had a floor covering and the fact that Pee-wee could not hear his own foot-falls agitated him strangely. Uncle Eb sat in the corner near the melodeon looking strangely out of place in his ticking overalls.

"Is—is she—dead?" Pee-wee whispered fearfully.

"Sit down, Walter," said Aunt Jamsiah; "no, she isn't dead, she's better."

Uncle Eb said nothing, only watched Pee-wee keenly.

Pee-wee seated himself, feeling very uncomfortable.

"Walter," said his aunt, "something very serious has happened and I'm going to ask one or two questions. You will tell me the truth, won't you?"

"I'll answer fer him doin' that," said Uncle Eb.

"Sure I will," said Pee-wee proudly.

"Walter, do you know what Pepsy's secret was? You remember she said she had a secret that would make lots and lots of people come and buy things from you?"

"Girls are—" Pee-wee began. He was going to say they were crazy, but remembering the one that lay upstairs he caught himself up and said, "they're kind of—they think they have big ideas when they haven't. I should worry about their secrets."

"But some of Pepsy's ideas and plans have been very big, Walter," his aunt said ruefully. "You see we know her better than you do. She's very, very queer; I'm afraid no one understands her."

"I understand her," said Pee-wee. "She believes in bad luck days."

Aunt Jamsiah paused a moment, considering; then she went straight to the point. "Pepsy wants to do right, dear, but she will do wrong in order to do right—sometimes. We have always been a little fearful of her for that reason. She—she can't argue in her own mind and consider things as—as you do."

"I know lots of dandy arguments," Pee-wee announced.

"You know, Walter, her father was a—he was a—not a very good man. And Pepsy is—queer. Last night she made a dreadful mess in the cellar. She was at the kerosene; oh, it makes me just sick to think of it. She had some rags soaked with kerosene. Some of them were found out by the well. The others—" Aunt Jamsiah lifted her handkerchief to her eyes and wept for a moment, silently.

"What others?" Pee-wee asked.

"The ones that were used to set fire to the bridge, dear. Oh, it's terrible to think of it. Poor, poor Pepsy. That is what is bringing lots and lots of people along our road to-day, Walter. Pepsy was found lying unconscious near the bridge. She had kerosene all over her. One charred rag was found over there. It just makes me—it makes me—"

Pee-wee arose and laid one hand on the back of the hair-cloth chair. He, too, was concerned now.

"You—you didn't tell her—you didn't blame—accuse her—did you?" he asked.

"No, I didn't," his aunt breathed worriedly.

"I asked her to tell me all about last night and she would tell me nothing. She said that the planks on the bridge tormented her. To almost everything I asked her she said, 'I won't tell.' She is very, very stubborn; she was always so."

"Because, anyway," Pee-wee said, alluding to his former query, "if anybody says she burned down the bridge on purpose it's a lie. I don't care who says it, it's a lie. She's—she's my partner—and it's a lie. If—even—if the minister says it, it's a lie!"

"Listen, my dear boy," said his aunt kindly. "I'm not angry with Pepsy, poor child. I'm not accusing her, and you mustn't talk about the Rev. Mr. Gloomer telling lies. Pepsy tried to burn down the orphan home once, for some trifling grievance. We can't take the responsibility of the poor child any longer. I'm afraid that any minute Beriah Bungel will want to take her—arrest her. I know she's your partner, dear, but it would be better for us to send her back to the state home where she will probably be kept than to let her be arrested. I don't think she knew what she was doing, poor, poor child—"

Aunt Jamsiah broke down completely, crying in her handkerchief. So Uncle Eb finished what little there was to say.

"We had to send fer 'em, Walter," said he. "She'll be better off there fer a spell, I reckon. I ain't so sure about her doin' it, though it looks bad. Least ways, she didn't know what she was doing. But don't you worry—"

Pee-wee did not wait to hear more. He just could not stand there.

"When—when are they—coming?" he asked. "I reckon to—morrow, boy. Now, you look here—."

But Pee-wee had gone.

Up the narrow, boxed-in stairs he went, never asking permission. He could see nothing but a big enclosed wagon, dark inside, with Pepsy inside it. He had no more idea what he was going to do that day than the man in the moon. But he knew what he was going to do that very minute. When a scout makes up his mind to do a thing. ...

Into the little room under the eaves he strode, his eyes glistening, but his heart staunch and his resolve indomitable. And she smiled when she saw him. She was sitting up and she looked ever so little in her nightclothes and ever so plain with her tightly braided red hair. But her eyes were clear and she smiled when she looked at him. ...

"I won't tell anybody where I went," she said, "because I was a smarty and I thought I could make somebody do a good turn ever so—ever so big. And they'd only laugh at me if I told them what it was. So I'm not going to be a tell-tale cat."

"Pep," he said, "it shows that you're right because lots and lots of automobiles are coming along our road since the old bridge burned down and it's a detour and that means hundreds and hundreds of them have to go past our refreshment place and we're going to make lots of money. And I thought of a dandy idea, it's what they call an inspiration. We're going to name the place Pepsy Rest, because Pepsy will remind people to buy chewing gum, because that has pepsin in it and as soon as you're all well we'll start in and keep on being partners, because we have a monopoly. Do you know what that is? It's when you can sell all you want of something and nobody else can sell it. ...

"Mr. Jensen, he put up a sign, and he said no one should sell things on his property and he owns all the property along the road, and you bet everybody is scared of him. So now we're going to have a great big business and we began as poor boys, I mean girls, I mean a boy and a girl. So don't you believe anything that anybody tells you, not even—not even Aunt Jamsiah. Because you know how I told you I was a good fixer and I'm always lucky, you have to admit that."

"Can I be the one to count the money?" Pepsy asked.

"Sure, and I'll be the one to eat what's left of the things that won't keep," said Pee-wee. "Only don't you worry no matter what you hear—"

She was on the point of telling him how Mr. Jensen had done his good turn after all, and all about what she remembered of the previous night. But she decided that she was not going to have a boy laughing at her and put it within his power to call her a tell-tale cat some day. So instead she threw her arms around him and said, "Oh goody, goody!"

You know how girls do.

CHAPTER XXXII

THE CLEW

Pee-wee never knew until now how much he cared about his little

companion of the summer and how little he cared about their roadside

enterprise except so far as she was concerned in it. All morning the

almost continuous procession passed along the road reviewed by a gaping

assemblage on the platform in front of the post office. Many motorists

who read the enticing promises along the way paused for refreshment only

to find the little rustic shelter bare and deserted.

But they were not the only ones to be disappointed. Upon the front porch of Doctor Killem's house there sat in a wheel chair the queerest little figure ever seen outside of a soup advertisement. He was of the kewpie type, all head and eyes, and he had a kind of ridiculous air of stern authority about him as he sat all bundled up in blankets soberly reviewing the passing cars. So odd and gnomelike was he that he might have stepped out of the pages of "Alice in Wonderland." He would have made a good radiator ornament on an automobile.

This, you will know, was little Whitie Bungel, who seemed not at all disconcerted at being elsewhere than in his own home. He had been moved about so much without any exertion on his own part that he was quite at home anywhere.

Though Pee-wee had spoken in high hope to Pepsy about their unexpected and glowing prospects, he was haunted by thoughts of the terrible thing which was to happen on the morrow. Pepsy was to be taken away, back to the big brick building which she hated, just as the planks of the old bridge had foretold;

Pee-wee's loyalty was so staunch that he did not even consider the things his aunt had said. He was going to save Pepsy from that place and make her the sharer of the fortune that was within their grasp. He made this resolve with the same generous impulse as that which had caused him to put two hundred and fifty dollars within the reach of Mr. Bungel who had boxed his ears.

"I'm lucky," he said to himself as he trudged down to the post office; "I'll fix things all right. I'll show them; I don't care, I'll show them. They won't take her back to that place, not while I'm around."

He did not know how he was going to prevent this but he had unbounded faith in his capacity to fix things and in his good luck.

So, as he trudged along, stepping out of the way of many cars, he came to the home of Doctor Killem.

"Hello, soldier," piped up a little thin voice upon the porch.

"I'm not a soldier," said Pee-wee.

"My father can arrest people," said the little gnome, looking straight ahead of him.

"That doesn't prove I'm a soldier," said Pee-wee.

"You've got a uniform," said the gnome. "I'm not afraid of soldiers. My father's got a lot of money, he's got two hundred and fifty dollars and I'm not going to get dead."

"Where's your father?" Pee-wee asked.

"He's up the road and he's going to catch people and put them in jail."

"Is he?"

"Why do you say 'Is he?' I didn't go to the hospital last night. Do you want to know why?" He asked questions as if they were riddles.

"Yes, why?" Pee-wee asked, half interested.

"Because the bridge burned down. Do you like bridges?"

"It isn't a question of whether a person likes them or not," Pee-wee said; preoccupied with his own sorrow and worry, yet amused in spite of himself at this queer little fellow.

"Yes it is," said Whitie Bungel.

"All right then, it is," said Pee-wee.

"Why did you say it wasn't?"

"Oh, I don't know, I guess I was thinking of something else."

"What were you thinking of?"

"Oh, I don't know—nothing."

"Why did you say you were?"

"You didn't tell me about why you didn't go to the hospital last night."

"I can see things that other folks can't see," Whitie announced.

"You're like Licorice Stick," said Pee-wee.

"He's black," Whitie said.

"I know he is."

"Then how am I like him? I'm white. My name is Whitie."

Pee-wee felt like a prisoner at the bar of justice with this little personage swathed in blankets, staring down at him. His wrappings covered his neck and all that could be seen of him was his face, perfectly motionless. Finally he said as if he were pronouncing sentence.

"Doctor Killem took me in his auto. We had to turn around and come back when we came to the bridge burning down. He's going to take me another way. I saw a man getting dead."

"Where?" Pee-wee asked, his interest somewhat aroused,

"Will you give me that tin thing if I tell you?"

"That isn't a tin thing, it's a compass, it tells you which way to go.

"Can it talk?"

"No, it can't talk."

"Then how can it tell you?"

"It points its finger."

"You're crazy."

"All right," Pee-wee laughed in spite of himself. "You tell me about the man getting dead and I'll give you the tin thing."

"He was lying down in the bushes and wriggling."

"Where? Near the bridge?" Pee-wee asked.

"Doctor Killem didn't see him and he laughed at me. He said I was seeing things. Can you wriggle? I looked back out of the window and saw him."

"Did you tell your father about it?" Pee-wee asked, hardly knowing what to think of this information.

"My mother made him give her the two hundred and fifty dollars so I wouldn't get dead. Do you know what I'm going to be when I grow up?"

"No; what?"

"A giant."

"Well, you'd better hurry up about it."

"Do you know where my father got that two hundred and fifty dollars?"

"Where?"

"It was a prize for catching thieves. You can't catch thieves."

"I know it," Pee-wee said.

"Are you going to be a thief when you grow up?"

"No, I guess not," said Pee-wee.

"You can have three guesses."

"All right, I guess not three times. Now, tell me if you told your father about seeing that man getting dead."

"Yes, and he said I'm always seeing things; everybody says that. Maybe I'll get dead when it rains."

"Don't you believe it," Pee-wee said; "Licorice Stick's been telling you that. Didn't you say you were going to be a giant first?"

"You're not a giant."

Alas, Pee-wee knew this only too well. He knew too that it would be quite impossible to get anything in the way of a connected narrative out of this stern little autocrat. Whether he had actually been "seeing things" or had only seen something in his queer little inner life, who should say? Evidently no one took him very seriously. And this fact did not seem to trouble him at all. Removing the compass cord from about his neck, Pee-wee advanced to proffer his second gift to the Bungel family. Little did that stiff, serious little figure know that the much-needed money which Mrs. Bungel had been wise enough to take from her husband, had come from the same source. Pee-wee searched in vain for any sign of hands in those enveloping blankets. There were no hands, there seemed to be no body even; just two eyes looking straight ahead as if their owner were not going to assist at all in the transfer of the little gift. So Pee-wee laid the compass on the porch rail.

"There you are," he said; "that needle always points to the north."

The two severe eyes stared down at the compass on the rail but their owner made no attempt to reach it as Pee-wee started off. If Pee-wee had not been so worried and preoccupied he would have thought that he had never seen anything so absurdly amusing in all his life.

"Come back and say good-by," the little voice commanded.

Pee-wee returned and stood in the exact spot where he had stood before and said, "Good-by." Although the little pale face did not turn the fraction of an inch, the staring eyes followed Pee-wee as he went along the road.

CHAPTER XXXIII

THE TRAMPLED TRAIL

Pee-wee felt as if he were emerging from some enchanted spot in the "Arabian Nights," abounding with giants and men "getting dead." He had no more belief in what this imperious little imp had told him than he had in the predictions of Licorice Stick, or the homely superstitions of Pepsy.

Indeed, if he had thought seriously of these erratic snapshot bits of information about figures wriggling in the dark and "getting dead" he would never have mentioned these things to Licorice Stick whom he ran plunk into as that aggregation of rags and nonsense sat upon a stone wall up the road engaged in the profitable occupation of watching the passing cars. Licorice Stick's business was contemplating the world and he always attended strictly to business.

"Lordy me!" he said, rolling his eyes, "you don' go nowheres that kid 'e tell you. Dat wrigglin' man, he no man, he a sperrit. Don' you go near dat bridge, you get a spell. Yo keep away f'm dat bridge."

How much this had to do with Pee-wee's actually going to the scene of the fire it would be hard to say. If he had not talked with Whitie he probably would not have gone. At all events, he had nothing else to do and he wanted to think. So he followed the trail through the woods to the highway.

It seemed quite probable that Whitie's jerky sentences were about true, that the doctor had been compelled to turn back by reason of the burning bridge. The fact that Whitie was holding his imperial court on the doctor's porch made this part of his story seem true.

Perhaps it would be about right to say that little Whitie's spasmodic announcements directed Pee-wee in his idle wanderings on that morning when he was fearful and sick at heart.

Long afterwards he remembered with interest that it was little Whitie Bungel (for whose recovery he had sacrificed two hundred and fifty dollars and not a little glory) who put him in the way of the terrible discovery that he made on that fateful day. And the funny thing about it was that the little gnome had given the clue to his benefactor and not his father who knew nothing about the frightful revelation of that morning until it was all over.

So perhaps there is a little god of good turns after all, who, all unseen, administers punches in the nose and pays back two hundred and fifty dollar gifts and so forth, and has the time of his life watching how these things work out. Or a "pay back sperrit" as Licorice Stick might have called him. ...

As Pee-wee approached the scene of the fire he saw in the bushes something which caught his eye. This was a torn fragment of clothing. The bushes were trampled down at the spot. It was not hard for the scout to follow this line of trampled brush which was so disordered that he thought it could not have been caused by a walking or fleeing person. It was well away from the area where the men had fought the flames.

Here and there something brown and sticky on the leaves caught the scout's eye. Some one had crawled stealthily through here. Or else dragged himself through. Pee-wee shuddered at this thought. He examined the trampled channel more carefully. And from this examination he was satisfied of one fact which made him uneasy, apprehensive.

The weight which had crushed the bush down had been a prone, dead weight. At intervals of perhaps three or four feet were gathered wounded strands of the tall grass, as if some groping hand had reached ahead, gathering and pulling on them. Pulling a helpless weight. Pee-wee knew this for he saw with the eyes of a scout.

CHAPTER XXXIV

THE TRAIL'S END

This trampled channel petered out in a comparatively bare area across which was more brush. Almost hidden in this was a tumbled-down shack, hardly bigger than a closet, in which boys who had been wont to dive from the old bridge had donned their bathing suits. It had been thrown together as a storage place for fishing tackle and crab nets and these latter, rotten and gray with age still hung in the dank, musty place.

Pee-wee paused a moment, irresolute, nervous. He had a strange feeling, a feeling of apprehension which amounted to a certainty. And as he paused two charred bits of timber from the old bridge, still held together by a rusty brace, creaked, and the creaking seemed loud in the stillness of desolation.

A rusty can, the discarded receptacle of bait, lay at his feet, and in his hesitation and transient fear, he kicked it, and followed it, kicking it again. Then, banishing such cracked-up excuses for delay he put aside his fears and went around the tiny shelter to where the rotted door hung loose upon one broken hinge.

Within lay a human figure. The hair was wet and matted and prickly leaves were stuck in it. The face was streaked with blood, the clothes were torn. One of the legs lay in a very unnatural attitude. The eyes were wide open and staring with a glassy look at some rough fishing rods which lay across the rafters above. One of the arms was outstretched and the hand lay open as if its owner were saying, "Here I am, you see." There was something very appalling about that dumb attitude of speech and welcome when the voice and the eyes could not speak. For he had "got dead," this poor troubled creature "got dead" after committing one hideous crime to hide another.

The people in the nearest house along the now deserted highway came at Pee-wee's breathless summons and gazed down silently but would not touch the figure with outstretched arm and opened hand that seemed to say, "Step in, you're welcome, here I am."

So they called the coroner and the body of Deadwood Gamely was borne away and it was soon known that he had died from injuries received in falling down the embankment which he was scrambling up after setting fire to one of the supports of the old bridge.

He had not done this horrible thing willfully, at least not for money to spend. That very day a warrant was issued for his arrest in Baxter City for embezzlement of funds which he had stolen from the bank in which he had been employed. But the angel of death had traveled faster than the law.

That the contractors, or one of them, who wished to benefit the county with a modern bridge had offered Gamely pay to do this dreadful deed of arson seemed certain. But it seemed equally certain that the wretched boy had balked at this frightful enterprise, putting it off from day to day, until discovery and arrest for his other crime stared him in the face. He had waited till the very night before the day on which his petty thefts would be revealed. Then in frantic desperation he had taken this only means of acquiring a sum of money quickly. No one could say this for a certainty.

But in a story where we have witnessed so many good turns may we not dismiss poor Deadwood Gamely and his tragic end from our thoughts with the hope, nay, even the confidence, that his second crime was not a deed of willing choice? There was more money misappropriated by Tom, Dick and Harry, before the new steel bridge was up than ever poor Deadwood Gamely, with his silly clothes and hat, would have dared to steal. And so the tax rate went up and Commissioner Somebody—or—other got a new automobile and County Engineer Grabson built a big house and so on, and so on, and so on.

But before the new million-dollar bridge was finished the Pepsy Roadside Rest was flourishing as the only real "monolopy" in Everdoze.

CHAPTER XXXV

EXIT

So it befell that the big black wagon belonging to the brick orphan home came and turned around and went back again. It got in the way of all the automobiles that were headed for The Home of Fresh Doughnuts (a new sign) and was a nuisance generally. The men who drove it didn't buy so much as a gumdrop.

But what cared the partners? For such a business were they doing as would make the Standard Oil Company turn green with envy. Their financial rating was so high that you couldn't see it without a telescope. Every time there was a strike over at the new bridge the partners reaped a profit from the delay. Thus labor unconsciously put business in the way of monopolies.

And so the great enterprise prospered. The advertising department had now two steady employees—Licorice Stick and Wiggle. Licorice Stick covered the road up as far as Berryville with a huge placard hung from his neck. Wiggle proudly flew an inflated balloon from his tail bearing the appropriate reminder HOT DOGS AT THE PEPSY REST.

One evening, oh, it must have been about six o'clock, the weary partners were closing up their little shack for the night. Pepsy was counting the money and Pee-wee was eating the cookies that were left over. For he was conscientious and must open shop with a fresh supply each day. Sometimes he would have a dozen or more to eat, but he did it bravely—from a sense of duty. A scout is dutiful.

Presently there hove in sight a large figure, walking.

"Oh, it's Mr. Jensen," said Pepsy; "hurry up and finish the cookies or he'll want them; he always does that."

Mr. Jensen came up mopping his forehead.

"Any lemonade left?" he asked.

"There's about one glass," Pee-wee said.

In accordance with his invariable daily custom, Mr. Jensen bought up the remainder of stock, drank several glasses of cider, and chatted with the partners.

"Ain't heard of any rivals, have you?" he asked. "We've got the whole detour eating out of our hands," said Pee-wee, which was literally true.

"Makin' money fast, huh? You takin' good care of this little gal of mine?"

Pepsy smiled at him and he put his arm around her and kissed her and said, "If he don't take good care of you, you just come and let me know."

Then he winked at Pee-wee.

When he was gone something reminded Pee-wee to look into the big lemonade cooler and make sure that it was empty. It was not quite empty, there being about ten lemon pits, a slice of rind, and a small piece of ice left in the bottom of it. But this was worth going after and Pee-wee went after it. With all his strength he raised the goodly cooler to a position above his head and tilted it to his mouth. His arms trembled under its weight, and his hands slipped upon its cold, beady sides. The several drops of highly diluted lemonade trickled down into his mouth but the flavory pits and rind remained at bay at the bottom of the cooler.

They would not roll but they might fall. Pee-wee held the cooler up to a perfectly perpendicular position above his upturned face. Then, oh, horrors! The wet cooler slipped through his hands and the curly head of Pee-wee Harris disappeared within it. If the postman who found him wrestling valiantly with a banana and clinging with the other hand, could only have seen him in this new and terrible predicament!

And thus the curly head and terribly frowning countenance of Scout Harris disappears out of our story into a new realm of joy. ...

THE END